Some bonds are stronger than blood.

When eighteen-year-old Ava and her boyfriend attend a party on campus, things turn from fun to deadly rather quickly. As Ava bleeds out on the concrete floor, the angel of death comes...only he's not an angel. And he isn't quite dead either.

Cassius Aurelia finds a young college student fighting for her life on the floor of a frat house basement, and he can't turn away. His bite will save her life, but it will also bring forth a litany of consequences for the both of them that neither may be ready for.

Blood & Bones

Ava Crowley, Vampire Slayer

Book One

Copyright ©2021 Ariel Dawn

ISBN: 978-1-77357-316-8

978-1-77357-317-5

Naughty Nights Press LLC

Cover Design by Willsin Rowe

DEDICATION

**I dedicate this book to all the
Avas of the world.**

Those who see the world beyond the veil.
Those who never back down from a fight.
The ones with a fire in their soul.
And also those who can't live without a
strong cup of coffee.

BLOOD & BONES

AVA CROWLEY

VAMPIRE SLAYER

BOOK ONE

ARIEL DAWN

NAUGHTY NIGHTS PRESS LLC • CANADA

CHAPTER ONE

AVA'S HEAD WAS *killing* her, and her bones literally ached like they'd been shut inside a coffin for a hundred years. She could hear the sound of the birds chirping outside her window, but they seemed so very loud it was almost comical. A wave of nausea overcame her, and she rushed to the bathroom. Her body heaved with convulsions as she emptied her stomach into the toilet.

Visions of the night slowly came back to her, coursing through her body.

The frat boys she and Ross were playing beer pong with.

Ross obliterated out of his mind, completely missing all his shots.

Ava and him making out in the basement.

Her senses felt heightened, as the loud incessant chirping sounded like nails on a chalkboard. Her stomach dry heaved, as the rest of the memories came forth.

The blood.

There was so...much...blood.

Her muscles ached, the vein deep in her thigh pounding with heaviness against her skin.

The feeling of the knife as it cut into her thigh like a knife cuts soft butter, the creamy texture making way for the impact of the steel.

The boy who'd been making eyes at Ross all night had him up against the wall, his lips on his neck, and Ross moaned with pleasure...before the scream.

The memory of his horrific scream...

Ava threw up again at the memory of his lifeless, drained body in the corner. Covered in blood. Her body shook with the leftover tremors from convulsions as another memory forged its way to the surface.

An angel emerging from the shadows, his glowing green eyes like a cat in the darkness. Like some kind of dream or hallucination...

How she pleaded for him to save Ross.

The sound of his voice, tender and beautiful, offering her a chance to live.

She pushed herself away from the toilet, scrambling back against the sink, the coolness of the pipes chilling the heat she felt within her. Her wrist throbbed with soreness, and she glanced down to see it wrapped in thick, white gauze, only the faintest hint of a lightly pink stain in the center.

The feel of absolute bliss as she watched the angel sink his teeth into her flesh.

The realization struck her, and she unraveled the gauze with a frantic, panicked motion. Her blood chilled as she stared at the bite mark, the raised scarring prominent as if she'd sustained the injury long before last night.

The searing pain as his tongue licked

at the wound.

Her stomach twitched at the memory, but it was not an unpleasant one.

"What the hell?" Her voice wavered aloud in the silence of the bathroom.

When she finally found the strength to move, she noticed the birds had stopped chirping, and her headache was gone.

CHAPTER TWO

"MUST HAVE BEEN one hell of a party last night." Ember pushed the paper cup full of sugary goodness toward Ava.

The campus was crawling with police and had turned into quite the crime scene.

Ava's stomach turned at the memory.

"You have no idea." Ava sipped the warm liquid, hoping it would settle her nerves, if only marginally.

The television reporter showed an image of Ross, with the subtitle *Missing twenty-year-old male, Ross Parish.* Ava's heart stilled at the sight.

They'd only been going out for a month. It just didn't seem real, the idea that their relationship was over before it even had a chance to begin. She was going to ask him to visit for Thanksgiving, for god's sake. If everything went smoothly.

Ross was dead, yet how could she describe what happened when she didn't understand it herself. Speaking up would only make her a suspect as she was the last person to see him alive. Her, and the freakishly beautiful blond man who bit her.

The words were solid in her brain

He fucking bit me. Maybe he was just

as tripped out as the rest of the frat boys.

She did remember the one biting Ross on the neck, and quite frankly he seemed pretty into it...until that point anyway. But when had things shifted? Everything was so blurry.

What kind of deranged person goes around biting people, let alone more than one? She thought as she watched Ross's picture on the scene.

Someone on drugs, most likely. She took another sip of her coffee.

"Did you see what happened?" Ember looked concerned.

"Not really, no," she lied. What could she say?

She looked down, catching sight of a familiar pair of eyes across the room

Bright, glowing green eyes stared at

her from across the student lounge, and her body went straight as a pole. Her wrist throbbed with a heated sensation, and she nearly dropped the cup of coffee.

"Ava, careful..." Ember leaned toward her, her fingers gently touching her forearm, focusing on the gauze.

"What happened to you anyway?" Her voice broke Ava's concentration.

"I'm not sure. I think I fell on some glass. I was pretty wasted, after all." At least it wasn't a *complete* lie.

"Well, I'm glad Ross had the wherewithal to make sure you were okay." She paused, a look of sorrow on her face.

"I'm sure he's okay. He'll turn up." Ava could see Ember's forced smile. Ember may have been psychic, but Ava knew her talents extended only to reading tarot, and not detective work like her aunt, the famous psychic consultant, Kacie Stone.

"Yeah. Sure," she said as she glanced around the quad, trying to find the green-eyed angel. But he was nowhere to be found.

Perhaps she was truly starting to lose her mind.

CHAPTER THREE

CASSIUS TOOK A deep breath as he made his way out of the student union, passing the young college students as if he were just another face in the crowd.

That was close. Perhaps she hadn't seen him.

She's all right. You can move on now. Forget about her. He walked with swift grace past a group of students coming through the turnstile doors.

The campus was as active as ever, but the news of the party was all throughout the town of Chester. He'd had to act quickly, with the rogue faction so close by, and he was certain they wouldn't be keen to have loose ends.

What was I thinking? He chastised himself. The memory of the night flooded back to him, with clarity.

Cassius followed Taj down to the basement. They weren't supposed to be in this part of the house, but Taj had a score to settle. No one threatened Jasmine and got away with it, especially some young, dumb new recruit. The Boracellis were either getting sloppy or desperate, or perhaps both.

After all Taj and Jasmine had done for him, there was no way he was letting Taj go off half-cocked without him. It wasn't that his friend couldn't stand off against the new kids; Taj was about as impenetrable as solid marble but the right crack in the right place could make him more than just distracted. Strength was his strong suit; brains.... Not so much.

The stairs creaked underneath him, and the scent of fresh blood assaulted his senses. He stilled momentarily, gaining his bearings. Taj brushed against his back.

"Do you smell that?" Taj whispered.

Cassius nodded.

His heightened sense of smell told him the room hadn't been cared for in some time as the scent of mildew and rotten beer permeated through the concrete like it had been there for years.

Taj sniffed the air behind him.

"I don't smell him. His scent's

disappeared," Taj grumbled angrily. Cassius could hear the creak of the stairs behind him, a clear indication his friend was turning around, heading back to the party.

"Please.... Help me..." The sound was small, and almost no more than a whisper. Cassius stepped forward.

"Cassius.... What the fuck? What are you doing?" Taj whispered.

The sight before him angered him in a way he hadn't felt in years.

Since Eden...

The bodies in the corner were piled like discarded packaging, and perhaps to the young vamps they were just that, but not all of them were lifeless shells.

The smell of coagulation was prevalent as he slowly walked toward the sound of the whisper, his gaze settling on its owner.

Her amber eyes were frantic with motion, until they settled on him. He glanced over her quickly, taking in the sight of the young college student who was sitting in a puddle of blood, streams of the crimson liquid seeping out from several gashes on her pale, sweat-slicked inner thighs.

No bite marks, which meant they hadn't fed off of her yet.

"Cassius, come on..." Taj stepped up toward the door, the tone in his voice only slightly worried. Cassius could smell the faint, distinctive smell of the young vamp. Young vamps thought their musk was alluring, and maybe it was to humans. But with his heightened sense of smell, it reminded him of humans who bathed in too much cologne.

"They're going to kill her." He turned toward the shadows where Taj was hidden.

He'd never understood, given the history of their relationships with the mortals, why some vampires preferred to be so cruel.

They'd worshipped their very existence, sacrificed themselves and everything they had once to be chosen, to be gifted with immortality. The humans gave them life, after all. Without their blood, they'd cease to exist.

The girl's chest heaved heavily, and her long, dark brown hair clung to her sweaty, dirty skin. He could feel her pulse like an echo in the air, even at a distance. The rush of blood in her veins. She would certainly bleed out soon if the rogue vamps didn't come back to finish *her off.*

She struggled to move her legs, frustration on her face. But she kept trying. "We're on their territory," Taj's voice went up an octave, and the reminder was sobering.

"My boyfriend, Ross...he's...he's still alive." Her voice was strong, even though it wavered with exhaustion. She looked into his eyes, and he was in front of her instantly.

He couldn't explain it, but when she looked at him, he felt...seen. Not as a vampire, not as an Aurelia but as a person.

He could not leave her to die alone, and he would not let her die at the hands of monsters, this human who tried with all her fading strength to move.

You're not a monster, he reminded

himself.

There wasn't much time to act as the sickeningly sweet scent of the young vampires became more prominent. They were getting closer, but the target was not with them.

He could turn her, it was the easiest option, but it would draw attention he didn't want from the Boracellis. Not as many vampires could turn humans anymore. It would be the most dangerous option, not to mention...

The idea of it didn't sit right with him. He'd never had a choice in the matter, he was born this way. He couldn't take the choice away from her. He knew all too well how it felt.

He could kill her, before the rogue faction showed up. He hadn't had fresh blood in many years, and he couldn't deny the sight of the crimson streaks against her pale thighs, streaming down her legs, was making his throat dry with thirst. It would be a quick, merciful death, thanks to his thrall, but he knew he'd never be able to do it. He'd never liked killing humans, even if he had to do it to survive. He'd managed to stay off of fresh blood this long, he wasn't going to throw all that discipline down the drain, even if it was tempting.

The only other option was, he could mark her. Marking her would buy more time. No vamp would dare try to challenge the claim unless they had a death wish, or unless they were stupid— like the rogue vamp who threatened Jasmine. The Boracellis wouldn't be able to do anything until he either turned her, or fed off her, for at least a few years. By *that time, she'd be graduated and likely out of Chester, and the Boracellis... He'd figure something out. He'd have to deal with them one day, after all.*

***

The sun was bright and warm, and Cassius started to feel the muggy effects of it against him. His vision blurred slightly, casting a fuzzy haze around the things he looked at, and the feeling of heat in his body flourished like the beginning of a summer bonfire. He wouldn't burn in the sun like the movies portrayed, after all, he needed to blend in with the humans, and his Aurelian blood gave him the ability to do so—but that didn't mean being out in daylight was comfortable by any means. While he'd spent much time outside in the sun in his early newborn days without any incident, the recent years of living in the night had caught up to him.

He walked through the crowds of students, toward the abandoned construction zone where the University suspended work due to lack of funding.

He knew not even students would be hanging out in its dusty, unkempt, forgotten rooms during this time of the day. It would be the perfect place to make an exit.

Cassius sat on the edge of the rafters. He'd had every intention of escaping quietly, but yet...

What if she saw me?

It isn't like she knows who you are, or what you are. If she's lucky she won't remember a thing thanks to the thrall, and she'll just chalk it up to drunken activities.

The vamps should leave her alone, with the mark...

He rolled the thoughts over.

Unless they're stupid. He reminded himself.

What had he done?

It seemed like the best option in the moment, he couldn't just *leave* her there to die at the hands of those horrible monsters. The choice seemed so simple, and yet, in the light of day, Cassius had to acknowledge that perhaps nothing was simple.

The memory of his fangs sinking into her skin... It had been so long since he'd felt the puncture of his teeth in real flesh, the rush of blood into his mouth. It was only a small taste, the blood that touched his fangs, and if he hadn't pulled back so quickly, he knew he would have been no better than the new recruits. But he couldn't deny the feeling of serenity as he drew her wrist to his lips, or the way his thrall instinctively wrapped itself around her, calming her fear and diluting the pain. The sound of her gasp, the feel of her pulse as it ran through him. The feeling of life in his hands, at his mercy.

He'd known marking her was the best option. It saved her life, sealing her wounds with rapid healing, and for that he knew he had made the right choice; but as he sat in the rafters, he could feel the faint thrum of her pulse inside his own veins, steady and strong, and for the first time in what seemed like an actual eternity, Cassius felt alive.

CHAPTER FOUR

EMBER TAPPED HER pencil on the table, and to Ava the sound was like nails on a chalkboard. It was like the sound was deafening.

"I swear to god, if you tap that pencil one more time, my head is going to explode," Ava grumbled.

Ember glanced up from her notebook with a mischievous smile.

Out of all the people in her Medieval

History class that she could have been paired with, she ended up with a psychic. An oblivious, anxious psychic. What were the odds?

Ava hugged her knees, her long, dark brown hair falling over her shoulders like a cascading waterfall. Her eyes focused on the group of students that hung around the Chester Cougar statue in the center of the quad. Something about them seemed familiar to her but she couldn't quite place it.

"Sorry." Ember glanced up at Ava quickly.

"No, I'm sorry. I just can't seem to shake this headache..." Ava massaged her temples with her fingers, squinting her eyes in the light.

"It has been three days." Ava watched the small group of students outside passing out flyers. Flyers with Ross's face on them. The group of students at the Cougar statue walked in their direction, and Ava could feel her skin prickle like she'd walked into a freezer. Her wrist heated underneath the gauze and she immediately let her legs down, bracing her hands on the bench.

It was as if time stood still and as the group approached, her eyes settled on one man.

He was average height, wearing an ordinary blue-checkered short sleeve over top of a white tee, and he looked like a California import. Tan skin, dark brown hair with blond highlights, and bright blue eyes.

As he passed her, her wrist felt a searing pain, and instinctively she grabbed the gauze with her free hand as their eyes met.

It was the guy from the party... The one who'd been making passes at Ross all night. The one who had him up against the wall... The one who bit him.

The man smiled seductively at her, and she could have sworn when his lips pulled back...

No, that can't be possible. You're definitely losing your marbles.

When his lips pulled back, she could have sworn she saw an elongated white, razor-sharp tooth.

A fang.

***

"Aren't you scared to go out after what happened?" Stacy looked up from the couch as Ava headed for the door.

"I need to get my mind off things,"

Ava answered plainly.

Stacy rose from the couch and walked over to Ava with haste. "I know you've had a tough week. With Ross missing, and I know the police interview you gave couldn't have been easy." Stacy ran her hand down Ava's exposed arm, her blue eyes full of concern.

Ava shifted out of her reach. Stacy sighed.

"I'm fine. It's not like we were soul mates or anything. Besides, I was glad to give that interview, if it helps find out who killed him." Her words weren't complete lies.

She'd met Ross at freshman orientation. He was a sophomore brother of Alpha Pi Omega, and he'd volunteered to help the freshman moving into the dorms. It wasn't fate or anything, he just looked really good moving boxes in his polo shirt and khakis, and Ava was excited to finally be able to do whatever she wanted, without judgment.

Like hit on a sophomore fraternity brother who was probably out of her league.

Only when Stacie's eyes widened had she realized her mistake.

"Killed?" Stacy swallowed, and Ava closed her eyes before opening them again. Her pulse quickened with anxiety.

"He's been missing for a week already, Stacy. If he were alive, they would have found him by now." She pursed her lips.

How has no evidence of what happened come to light?

The image of the California import flashed in her mind

His body pressed against Ross, his fingers on his neck.

Ross's moan of pleasure.

Ross's scream of pain.

His body behind her, the sound of gurgling blood.

The angel from the darkness...

She had awakened in her own dorm room...

What had they done with Ross's body?

The memory of the blood covering his shirt, trickling onto the cement floor...

Ava pushed the memory down. She could really use a drink.

Stacy crossed her arms. "You're not going alone." She spoke with confidence.

"I'll be fine," Ava replied quickly.

"I'll go with you," Stacy said as she stepped in between Ava and the door.

"Give me five minutes to change." She looked Ava in the eye with a look that said she meant business.

Ava sighed heavily. "Fine." she relented.

Ava leaned herself into the passenger seat of Stacy's bright blue Malibu. Her roommate's car always smelled like laundry detergent, and it was both a welcoming smell and a sickening smell at the same time. Ava stifled a cough.

Stacy turned the car on and backed out seamlessly.

"Where to?" She glanced at Ava.

"The Heights," Ava responded.

The Heights at Chester University wasn't actually affiliated with the school, which made it the prime spot for parties and underage drinking. It was also on the other side of the University, far away from Greek Row.

Stacy pulled up to the parking lot across the street from The Heights, the one everyone parked in to avoid getting a ticket.

It looked as if the party was stretched all throughout the parking lot, and in various apartments. Ava exited the car, the chilly October air biting at her bare legs. She pulled at her red velvet dress for a fraction of warmth as her long hair blew in the wind, tendrils sticking to her lip gloss and blinding her vision.

She swatted at her hair with disdain as she followed Stacy across the street to The Heights.

CHAPTER FIVE

TAJ LICKED HIS lips as a group of college students passed. The scent of chemical vanilla and freesia made Cassius's eyes water.

"We're not here for them," he reminded him.

"You might be a fucking vegetarian, but some of us still require the real thing to live." He leaned against the wall, holding his red solo cup and Cassius had to admit Taj looked like he belonged.

Tajiri's normally long, dark brown hair was pulled back into a tight bun, the style showcasing his high temples, and muscles in his neck. The black Billabong shirt that he deliberately wore was so tight; if he were human, it would have cut off his circulation. The fit made his profound muscles stand out, and that was, of course, on purpose.

A short, petite blonde with cerulean eyes walked up the counter, eyeing up the many bottles, cans, and strewn debris of plastic cups.

Taj's eyes lit up.

"Did it hurt?" He smirked as he pushed off the wall, slowly boxing her in.

Cassius rolled his eyes.

The doe eyed blonde flashed her long eyelashes at him.

"Excuse me?" Her voice was light.

"Did it hurt? When you fell from heaven?"

Cassius turned with every intent to leave, but a solid force stopped him dead in his tracks. Aside from the force of body collision, Cassis felt a strange, heated sensation in his veins. *Warmth...*

His slow heartbeat beat only a fraction quicker, and he could *feel* the thrum of pulse steady like a river inside his entire body.

"I'm sorry," the voice apologized.

Cassius looked down to see the culprit, and if he had human blood, he was sure it would have run cold.

The girl from the basement.

The one he marked.

For the first time in his eternal life, Cassius was speechless.

She looked up at him, and he had to take in the beauty of her amber colored eyes. Flecks of gold in them reminded him of the sun. She brushed past him as if he didn't exist, heading straight toward the blonde who was now running her fingers down Taj's enormous bicep.

He watched as the girl from the basement, the girl he *marked,* walked through the kitchen. She wore a short, red velvet dress, which elongated her pale legs, and the image of her on the floor, with crimson streaks against her flesh, flared his thirst, among other things.

Good thing I stopped at the morgue first. Something about this human… made him long for the taste of fresh blood in a way he hadn't felt in years.

The blonde saw her friend, and gave

Taj a playful shove as the marked girl took her arm and lead her away into the crowd on the other side of the kitchen, in the thick of the living room.

And just like that, she was gone, and the scent of sickening cologne became more prevalent. Taj's stance shifted in response, and Cassius remembered why they came to The Heights in the first place.

Forget about her. You've done your part. She's alive.

But even as he said the words in his head, he could feel her pulse inside of him and he knew forgetting her was out of the question.

CHAPTER SIX

AVA'S SKIN WAS chilled, and her wrist flared with heat as if it were on fire.

She grabbed the silver cuff and turned it against her bite mark, the scar that didn't seem to want to heal despite how much Neosporin she put on it. The cool metal of the silver didn't seem to help as it only heated up in response.

She looked down briefly and ran into a brick wall.

A brick wall wearing black leather pants, and...black and white converse tennis shoes?

What an odd combination.

She looked up the tall expanse of the said brick wall, and her heart stopped.

The angel from the shadows. From the party. The one who bit her.

She cleared her throat.

A thousand words assaulted her senses. A part of her wanted to scream at him, a part of her wanted to thank him, and a part of her wanted to ask him if he knew what happened to Ross's body.

But all she could manage was, "I'm sorry."

She shoved the thoughts down, her fingers pressing against her bite mark on her heated wrist.

She looked up at the angel of darkness for only a moment, taking in the sight of his beauty in the filtered light of the kitchen. His features truly were angelic.

His eyes were the brightest green she'd ever seen, like emeralds, and his golden blond hair was medium length, long enough to sweep back behind his ears and short enough that it barely touched his eyes. He looked like some lost member of the Backstreet Boys mixed with the god Apollo. The sight of him stirred a strange feeling inside of her she couldn't quite place.

She pushed past him and made a beeline for Stacy, who was flirting with some guy who was more muscle than human.

She grabbed Stacy by the arm and

pulled her away, and as she walked toward the living room, her heart stopped again.

In the center of the room was the group of students from the cougar statue. The California import stood in the center, with his red solo cup, laughing as though he had not a care in the world.

The images of the party from that night flooded her brain again.

His body on top of Ross's.

The moan of pleasure.

The scream of pain.

Ava's blood boiled.

The smile he cast in her direction, the memory of a long, sharp fang she thought she saw.

Her wrist still flared with heat, and she could see the goosebumps on her arm.

His eyes settled on her, and she investigated them from across the room and all she could see was emptiness.

He nodded in her direction, raising his cup to her.

Ava felt her legs move in his direction as if willed by some unknown force. Her eyes felt heavy, and her body felt strange.

I've only had one drink...

Perhaps someone spiked the punch with some kind of drug...

Her brain felt fuzzy.

Ava watched as someone approached California. His gaze still fixated on her as the other guy whispered something in his ear.

California broke eye contact and turned away, his expression turning to concern.

Ava's skin still prickled like ice, and her wrist still flared with heat, but her eyes felt alert, her brain less fuzzy, and she couldn't quite remember the walk from the kitchen to where she stood. When she looked up, California was gone.

CHAPTER SEVEN

TAJ SLAMMED HIS fist into the punching bag in the gym. "We almost had him!" he growled as his fist thudded against the oversized sandbag.

Cassius sat on the bench like a statue.

"Perhaps we would have had him if you kept your eye on the prize," Cassius retorted.

"Fuck you." Taj pounded into the

punching bag again.

"Just saying," Cassis sarcastically responded.

"I was hungry. Some of us *do* actually still need to eat, you know." Taj stilled the punching bag for a moment.

"I get thirsty too. I just have more control than you." Cassius pushed himself off the bench and walked over toward the window. The moon was high in the sky tonight.

"I have control," Taj grumbled. "At least we know their hunting grounds now."

Cassius stared at the silver moon, his mind replaying the night that changed his life.

The way she tried to move her legs.

Her eyes as she begged him for help.

The sound of her voice as his fangs

punctured her skin

The feel of her pulse alive within him.

He shook his head and pushed away from the window. "True. But I still feel guilty we couldn't catch him in time." He sighed.

"This isn't about Liam, is it?" Taj walked over to him.

"I saw her. The girl I marked." He turned toward Taj.

"The brunette that stole my dinner? Thought she looked familiar," Taj's words were careful.

"You ever mark anyone Taj?" Cassius asked honestly.

Taj removed the gauze wrappings from his knuckles slowly and methodically.

"A long time ago," he answered quietly.

"What happened?" Cassius swallowed.

"I killed her. Obviously. Man's gotta eat."

Cassius closed his eyes. He knew the answer, but hearing it aloud made it real. Taj couldn't sire newborn vampires. He didn't have the ability to turn humans as Cassius did.

"Why did you mark her?" he asked.

"Her blood...it was like it called to me. I *needed* it...and honestly..." Taj paused before continuing. "To this day it was the sweetest blood I've ever had."

Cassius could see the lust in his eyes at the memory of its taste. "Well, I don't intend on killing her." He turned his gaze back out the window.

"Then *you've* only got one other option." Taj flexed his fingers and

Cassius could see it in the reflection of the windowpane.

Marking a human meant Cassius had claimed her blood for his own use. If he turned her...one bite would spread the venom, and she would be like him. Frozen forever in her youth, with only one true desire. Blood.

Drinking her blood and spreading the venom through the bite...would make her his mate for life. She'd have to bite him after her transformation to solidify the bond but...

No.

Cassius forced the thought down. He'd vowed never to claim a mate, not after everything had crumbled with Eden. He'd come so close to bonding with her...

The memory of Eden Boracelli

surfaced, and he had to fight its pull.

The girl struggled in his grasp, and Eden held her still.

"Use your thrall." She instructed him. Her dark blue eyes instilled him with confidence.

Cassius tried to control the thrall, imagine it like some invisible force as Eden had told him. He imagined the invisible force like a shield around the girl. She looked at him with pleading eyes, and her breath hitched.

Eden sunk her teeth into the girl's neck, the sound of crunching muscle and torn tendons sending a shiver through his body. He could hear her heartbeat, feel it like a vibration of bass. The girl rolled her head back, her moan of pleasure a melody of its own.

Cassius was next to her in an instant,

his hands braced on top of her heaving chest, her heartbeat thudding against his touch. His lips barely brushed her skin before his fangs punctured the other side of her neck. The feeling of blood as it ran down his throat, hot and wet, was overpowering. Intoxicating.

He glanced at Eden, who licked the blood off her lips, and his heart swelled at such an intimate moment.

He pushed the memory down, as he hurried out of the gym.

"Where are you going?" Taj asked.

Jasmine came into sight, and Cassius felt his speed kick in involuntarily. His mind raced with thoughts and he needed to quiet them.

The streets of Chester were quiet everywhere, but the campus and Cassius found solace on the main street, under the streetlights. He sat on a bench and watched the flickering of neon on the sign of Cory's Diner, focusing on the buzzing sound from the wires inside of it.

The faint thrum of a pulse, steady and warm filled his body and he reveled in its warmth.

CHAPTER EIGHT

THE NEWS HADN'T forgotten about Ross, but he was only a footnote now that two girls had been found dead in one of the apartments in The Heights. The campus was aflutter with gossip and news of the horrific murder was hard to avoid.

Danica and Riley Klume, twin sisters were found in their apartment and had died of blood loss.

The strange thing was...

Except for two puncture marks on their bodies—one on Danica's neck, and one on Riley's inner thigh—there were no wounds or cuts to explain the loss of blood.

Ava felt overwhelmed. Chester U hadn't had a student death in over fifty years. Until her first semester. Not to mention, the constant feeling as if she was being watched...

Ava wasn't a paranoid person, but she still couldn't shake the feeling. Sometimes she'd look up and swear she caught a glimpse of glowing green eyes.

Ember pushed the paper cup of coffee toward her. "Drink up, we've got a lot of ground to cover," she said sweetly.

Ava grabbed the cup, glancing at her wrist. It had been two weeks since the day she received the bite, and it had become a permanent scar. Thankfully, she could cover it up with concealer or jewelry, but it still bothered her.

Her phone rang, interrupting their study session, and Ava was surprised to see the caller. She answered quickly.

"Mal?" Her voice lit up.

"Hey, Simba, how's college life treating you?" The sound of her brother's voice was remarkably refreshing.

"Well, it hasn't been quiet up here, that's for sure." She looked at Ember, and motioned to her she'd return in a moment. Ember nodded and Ava pushed herself away from the table in the quad and walked outside.

The sight of the autumn leaves as they scattered the green grass was comforting as the chill set in. Ava pulled on her grey sweater, the cuff itching her bite scar.

"I heard. That's kind of why I'm calling. I'm stopping home for a bit, and I'd like to see you if that's okay?" Ava could hear the concern in his voice, but he masked it as a question and not a command. She knew him better than that.

"Where are you?" she asked.

"In the parking lot of Grayson Building C," he said plainly.

"Let me wrap up this session with my partner, and I'll be right over," she answered with a smile.

"Sounds great," he said.

She couldn't wait to see her brother.

CHAPTER NINE

AVA WALKED UP to the familiar red Chevelle, and her brother smiled at her from inside the car. "You hungry?" He raised his eyebrow at her.

She came around to the passenger side, pushing her long hair back behind her. "The question is not am I hungry…" she said as he pushed the door open for her from inside. "The question is can I eat food? And to that you know the answer is most certainly always yes." She smiled back at him.

Mal turned the car on, and Ava had to admit, she wondered where Mal would have fit in at Chester U. The eleven years between them should have separated them more than it did, but Ava had always felt closer to her brother than anyone, including her parents.

Especially after they died.

The thought careened through her brain, and she frowned.

It was only three years ago...

She tried to push the memory away. She didn't want to remember the sight of her parents when she came home, their lifeless bodies strewn about on the carpet, saturated in blood in their home. She closed her eyes and tried to imagine anything else.

"Place is a freaking nuthouse with all these reporters and police everywhere," Mal said as he pulled out of the parking lot onto the road.

Ava opened her eyes and let out a deep breath. "Yeah, well, you know how it is. Nothing interesting ever happens around here, so can't say I blame them for all the attention." She leaned back into the squeaky leather seats.

"So, what's good up this way?" He leaned back casually as he palmed the steering wheel, turning onto the main street of the campus.

"Depends, what are you hungry for?" she asked as she peered in the back seat at the amp and guitar that looked as if they had collected dust.

Strange for a musician.

She looked up briefly to see Mal's

eyes in the rearview mirror, staring back at her.

"Pizza?" His tone was casual, but his eyes serious. Something about him seemed on edge.

Of course, he's on edge. His baby sister is attending a university where three people were just murdered.

"There's Julian's a couple of blocks from here. Just keep going straight until you hit the traffic light, then turn right on Tucker," she directed Mal.

His gaze turned back to the road.

"Did you know them?" he asked as they pulled up to the traffic light, which changed from yellow to red.

"What?" She turned toward him, with question.

"The...victims. Did you know them?" The way he said the word *victims* didn't sit right with her. She shrugged it off. "I knew the guy. Ross Parish." She spoke honestly.

"I'm sorry." His sympathy sounded genuine, but the look in his eyes was still quite serious. The light blinked green.

Ava pulled at the cuff on her sweater, covering her wrist.

"We only went out a couple times. He was a sophomore. Member of Alpha Pi Omega." It felt good to be honest with someone.

"So... you didn't know the girls then?" He turned right on Tucker Street.

Why was he pressing about this?

"No." Her answer was simple.

"Look, Ava, I know college can be exciting, what with all that goes on up here..." he started as he drove down the street, looking for the sign for Julian's. Ava shifted in her seat uncomfortably.

Please don't try to be the responsible older sibling. It just isn't you, Mal.

"So...you came all this way to lecture me?" She huffed.

Mal, of all people, had no room to lecture her. She wasn't some naive kid. She knew all too well what kind of shenanigans he got up to when he traveled for his gigs.

"I was eighteen once too. I know what happens at college parties. I also know that your friend and those girls were at a party the night they died." His lips straightened.

Ava shrugged as Mal parked the car.

"I'm fine, Mal. Really. You don't need to worry." She opened the door as quickly as she could. Her stomach growled.

"I'm not telling you not to do it. I know you're going to. I'm just telling you to be smart." He shut the car door and leaned against the hood of the Chevelle, as he took out a cigarette from his flannel pocket. He lit it with a stainless-steel lighter and the motion as he did so exposed his pentagram sun tattoo on his forearm, the rays of the sun sticking out like black daggers. Ava pulled her sweater tight around her.

"Finish your cigarette. I'm hungry," she grumbled.

Mal blew a ring of smoke in the air, and just like that the serious tone was gone, and his eyes lit up with a smile. "As you wish, Miss Crowley."

***

Ava closed her eyes and let a small moan of appreciation escape her lips. The cheese was absolutely delectable. "They really do have the best pizza," she mumbled through a mouth full of food.

Mal seemed to be on edge, his gaze darting around the room. It was only a Tuesday night, and still early by campus time, but fall had started to set in, and the outside was bathed in darkness, save for the streetlights and lights from places like Julian's.

Mal picked up another slice of pizza from the platter and scarfed it down equally as quickly as he had the other three slices.

The door jingled and Ava felt the familiar prickling of flesh and heated sensation at her wrist.

She looked up to see a group of

students filing into one of the booths. California was with them. He sat with his posse, which consisted of three other men, all of which were impeccably dressed even for brothers of the fraternity.

Mal's gaze darted over to them.

"You know those guys?" he asked between bites.

"Not really, just seen them around campus. I think they belong to Alpha Pi Omega." She took a sip of her coke and tried to ignore the chills.

Probably some stupid flu.

California locked eyes with her and nodded back at her.

"That the fraternity your friend was from?" Mal asked as he took another bite of cheese pizza.

Ava nodded in response. "Yeah." Her

head felt fuzzy again.

"Interesting," Mal said under his breath. Ava broke eye contact with California and shook off the feeling. She pretended not to hear him.

CHAPTER TEN

TWO GIRLS. IN addition to the boy at the frat house, Liam, the Boracelli's newest member, had managed to kill two innocent girls. Cassius was furious at the sight of what the news called The Chester Murders. They'd been killed at the off-campus housing complex, known as The Heights, or rather the apartment complex that they had visited two weeks ago, on the hunt for Liam.

Jasmine had told Taj to let it go. She didn't think Liam would do any harm. "It's just words, Taj. Seriously. He's a kid, let it go," she had said sweetly, but Cassius knew Taj better than Jasmine.

Liam was a baby as far as vampire years were concerned. He'd been turned within the last twenty years, and as Cassius had learned, been sired by a rogue vampire, which in itself was quite a rare occurrence. Rogues didn't usually have the ability to sire as their bloodlines were usually so diluted. Liam had no coven, no real understanding of rules, and yet the Boracelli's took him into their coven, likely because he was racking up quite the body count—which was something the Boracelli's favored above all else. Kills. If the rumors were true, he'd be an apprentice before the fifty-year mark. He'd only surfaced in Virginia a month ago, and already in the course of two weeks, he'd managed to kill three students at the campus. All Greek row, all in their early twenties.

Like him.

It could have been four. He reminded himself as he felt the faint thrum in his veins of a pulse that didn't belong to him.

Still, newborn vamps like Liam were arrogant and didn't understand how to blend in. Their cocky attitudes coupled with the new fondness of eternal life meant sometimes they drew too much attention, where there should have been none.

Taj walked through the parking lot, and his whistle pulled Cassius out of his thoughts.

Taj walked around the red Chevelle and licked his lips. "They just don't make them like this anymore, do they Cassius?" Taj sounded like he'd fallen in love.

The red paint shimmered in the streetlight, casting a glare.

"Not really my type." He shrugged.

Taj flipped him off.

"You wouldn't know taste if it walked up to you and bit you," he retorted.

Cassius noticed something catching a glare from the light, the sparkle glinting against the window.

He peered in the backseat and felt an immediate fear.

The source of the glare belonged to the expanse of a blade, made of what Cassius assumed to be pure silver, its markings all too familiar.

To the naked eye it looked no different than a hunting jackknife, but any vampire worth his blood knew it was anything but ordinary. The symbols etched into the pure silver blade were deadly to his kind.

"Taj, look. Back seat." He shoved his hands into his pockets as he stared at the blade.

"Fucking hunters. Great," Taj cursed.

Cassius could feel the stolen pulse in his veins quicken, and a chill came over him.

What the hell...

He pulled his hand out of his pocket, the feeling of fire dull at his wrist, but noticeable enough to make him jump.

"You alright over there?" Taj walked hastily over toward him.

"Yeah... I..." Cassius flexed his

fingers. He could feel the quickening heartbeat, and he knew it wasn't his.

"Lovely." Taj looked in the opposite direction, his sights settling on Julian's.

"What..." Cassius's thoughts felt jumbled.

Taj pulled him closer to the edge of the parking lot.

Cassius felt the pulse become stronger. "What is this? What is happening to me?" he asked.

"It's the mark. It knows she's close." Taj dropped his hand and nodded in the direction of Julian's.

Cassius's own heart stilled, which was a feat considering it was a slow beat to begin with.

She sat there in front of the window, with a dark-haired man, eating cheese pizza.

But it wasn't the sight of her that stilled his heart, not entirely.

It was the sight of Liam and his three henchmen, who walked in the door of Julian's.

CHAPTER ELEVEN

MAL PULLED OUT his wallet and fished around for the proper bills and change. The motion was normal, but his demeanor seemed to have changed. Ava finished the last slice of pizza and took another swig of her coke, and when she looked up California was beside the table.

"I know this may seem a bit forward, but you look awfully familiar to me. Do I know you?" California's voice didn't *sound* like a regional surfer, but more like a Tiffany Jewelry salesclerk. Combined with his preppy style, and expertly styled coif of hair, Ava couldn't help but blush.

Her brain felt fuzzy again, and the chills were still there, and she knew this man...but...

She didn't seem to remember *how.*

That's strange...

"I think so, but forgive me... I can't remember how." She glanced at Mal who's face had gone stone cold as he stood up slowly, against one of the other men who refused to move.

"Back off," he growled.

The man against Mal was wearing a pink polo of all things, and khakis with boat shoes. His backward hat looked slightly out of place with the rest of his ensemble and his dark eyes looked excited as he chewed his lip.

"Looking for a fight, pal?" Pink Polo challenged.

California held his hand out.

"Not tonight, Brody. Take it easy. You need your strength," he continued to speak, never taking his eyes off Ava.

"Well, then I think we should introduce ourselves thoroughly. I'm Liam Bancroft." He smiled, and although her brain felt hazy, she found her eyes had resisted the heavy pull.

"Ava Crowley," she smiled. Something about California...no *Liam's* demeanor felt unbelievably captivating. Memories of lips on her skin, biting at her flesh...

Biting...

Ava blinked and looked down to her

wrist for only a second, remembering what lay underneath her sweater. She tugged at the cuff, as something told her she needed to keep it hidden.

The door jingled, and Liam and Brody turned their heads.

"Back up right now, or I will make you," Mal sneered at Brody as he puffed his chest out.

Liam sighed. "Can't a guy just get a decent pizza around here without getting into an argument?" He looked back at Ava, and she cracked a smile.

"See you around, Ava." He smiled in return, his lips pulling back just enough that as he turned, Ava could have sworn that she saw it.

The razor-sharp fang.

Just like in the field.

Liam and Brody backed away slowly

as they headed toward the door, and Ava was surprised to see no one was there.

How odd. She thought to herself as she looked out the window.

Where Brody and Liam should have been, there was no one. Not a soul on the street, across the street, or anywhere to be found where a person should be.

Mal's shoulders eased, and he shot Ava a serious glance.

"You're coming home with me tonight." The way he said the words was definitive, and solid.

"What? Why? There's absolutely..." she started to rattle, but Mal held his hand up to stop her.

"I'd just feel better if we were both under the same roof. I'll drop you off at class tomorrow. I'm not going anywhere anytime soon." He stood in front of her, his eyes serious as he waited for her to rise.

"You're being ridiculous, but I can see that you are clearly worried. If it makes you feel better, I'll come home for a few days, but I'm a freshman. I can't have a car on campus, so I'll need you to drive me to and from school for the foreseeable future until you are satisfied. Also, we'll need to stop by my dorm to get a few things." She crossed her arms.

"Always the negotiator," Mal smiled only a fraction as he turned toward the door, and Ava followed.

Stacy's eyes sparkled at the sight of Mal, and Ava's stomach turned with disgust.

"You didn't tell me you had a brother. A very *hot* brother, I might add," Stacy whispered as Ava threw some clothes in her duffel bag.

"My brother is not hot, by any definition of the word, and most certainly is not suitable dating material. He's a musician, and therefore leaves for long periods of time, and isn't exactly the committed type." Ava wrinkled her nose.

"Like I said. Hot." Stacy shrugged.

"He's at least eight years older than you, Stacy." Ava strung up her laundry bag full of clothes she'd planned on taking to the Laundromat before Mal showed up.

"Age ain't nothing but a number, sweetheart. Besides you have room to talk. Wasn't your boyfriend two years older than you?" Stacy sat on her bed on the opposite side of the room, in crossed leg position as Ava went about packing her things for a few nights. She banked that Mal would get sick and tired of playing responsible sibling after three days. He didn't know how to stay in one place too long, anyway.

"Yeah, but that's different." She dodged Stacy's disapproving glare.

"No, it isn't," Stacy teased.

Ava slung the bag over her shoulder and headed for the door, the laundry bag at her side.

"Okay Mal, I'm ready. Let's head out. I've got class at eight am tomorrow," she said as she threw the laundry bag into Mal's stomach, the motion making him wince.

Mal coughed.

"Jesus Ava, what do you have in there? Bricks?" he retorted as Ava walked quickly out of the dorm room.

"Bye, Stace!" she hollered from the

hall, and Mal skipped after her.

CHAPTER TWELVE

MAL PULLED THE car into the driveway of the estate, the headlights casting an eerie white-blue glow on the stone walls. If it was up to Connie, their housekeeper slash pseudo mother, Ava would have remained living at the estate instead of on campus at Chester U for her first semester.

But with Mal gone most of the time, and the rigid structure of their aunt and guardian, Becky Lee Michaels, Ava knew she couldn't stay, even if the estate was a hundred times nicer than her dorm room. Not to mention, cleaner.

"Quiet, or you're going to wake the dead," Ava said as she tiptoed to the porch, waiting for Mal.

Mal fished for the right key on the ring.

"Relax. I called earlier today and told her I'd be stopping home for a bit," Mal replied as he found the key and turned it in the lock.

The click was an ominous sound to Ava, who suddenly worried why she'd agreed to this arrangement in the first place. She *was* perfectly capable of taking care of herself.

"Yes, but I'm sure you didn't mention I'd be coming with you." Ava crept in the open door, glancing around the darkened kitchen, waiting for Becky to show up out of nowhere, like some ghost.

"It's fine, don't worry about it. I'm sure if you tell her you feel safer here, she won't object. It *is* your home, Ava." Mal shut the door and locked it quickly.

Ava glanced at the grandfather clock in the living room, which read ten thirty pm. It wasn't even eleven and the house was already asleep.

When Ava turned the light on in her room, she was surprised to see it was just as she'd left it. The bed was still haphazardly made, the remaining pillows strewn about as if she'd taken a nap, and awakened. Yet, the room was devoid of all its charms as she'd taken the only things she valued with her to college. Her favorite band tees, her records and record player, and of course her tiny collection of paranormal books, and her dream catchers.

Mal dropped her bag on the floor, and it landed with a thud. "It's late, I'm going to turn in," he said quietly.

"I have class at eight, so we'll need to leave around six-thirty." The way she spoke was a command, not a question.

Mal sighed. "Alright. Get some rest." He turned, pausing in the doorway as if he wanted to say something. When the moment passed without a word, Mal shut the door, and Ava suddenly felt exhausted.

Flashes of light flickered in the darkness.

The light from the tiny sliver in the wall.

A door.

Ava wanted to move, but her legs were heavy.

Ross's eyes darted to the light, and all Ava could see was the look of lust.

What had him so worked up?

Why couldn't she move?

The shadows faded into the familiar muted green and beige wallpaper she'd always hated back when living in Loxley, Massachusetts. Ava quietly pushed on the open door.

The sink was running, and the kitchen was empty.

The Record player was still playing Aerosmith, and Ava could tell by the melody it was Sweet Emotion.

"Mom? Dad?" she called out.

But there was no answer.

And there never would be.

It had been weeks since Ava had the nightmare about her parents. She thought perhaps she'd finally outgrown them, or perhaps the dream catchers had worked. But as she tossed and turned, her body heated with anxious sweat, and she reached out into the empty space, searching for something that was not there.

Green eyes gazed down at her, and delicate fingers held her wrist. "I need your permission." His voice was like chocolate ganache on a chocolate donut. Smooth, and decadent.

Ava didn't understand. What was he waiting for? Couldn't they just leave... Surely, he could support her until she found her footing. Her head swelled with a blissful calm and her stomach flipped. She could feel her breathing increase, her heartbeat thudding in her chest, and the feeling of wanting to be consumed, wanting his touch...

The memory of razor-sharp fangs...

Ava awoke in a panic as Mal banged on the door.

CHAPTER THIRTEEN

CASSIUS WALKED AIMLESSLY along Chester's Main Street. The cool air felt refreshing against his skin, contrasting the slight warmth beneath it that didn't belong to him.

Not even corpse blood made him feel this warm.

He ran his hand through his hair, and when he pulled his fingers away, he could feel tiny beads of sweat.

Sweat?

Cassius couldn't remember the last time he felt so warm. The faint thrum in his veins, his pulse—*her pulse*—he reminded himself. It felt...

Heightened.

Cassius stopped for a moment and rescinded his movement. The fainter it became.

He walked quickly, and the thrum became more evident.

The memory of earlier that night resurfaced.

"It knows she's near," Tajiri said.

Cassius followed the feel of her pulse.

Is she in danger?

Is it Liam?

A strange feeling of possession and panic overcame him, and the world around him was nothing but shadow, and the light that drew him was not really a light at all.

Cassius stopped outside a large estate. It wasn't unusual to see a converted plantation home in Virginia, but there weren't many in Chester. The town itself wasn't really large, and was more spaced out, more country than city.

It was why he had stayed. Eden would never think to look for him in a secluded, small country town.

But now...

As long as I don't turn her or consume her blood...they won't be able to do anything. At least...not for a few years.

A few years. That's all he'd have to figure a way out of this. If he could just make sure the girl was alright...

Cassius's legs moved of their own

accord as he pushed through the iron gate to the estate.

Her pulse increased.

Cassius followed its call, like a sailor lured by a siren and stopped outside a large window.

He could see rather well in the dark; a trait he'd inherited from his father.

There was no danger.

She lay in bed, tossing and turning as if...

As if she's having a nightmare. He sighed.

It was at that moment he noticed her window was not completely shut.

Cassius stood there for a moment, his brain at some sort of crossroads.

Just shut it, and leave.

She's fine.

You're overreacting.

This mark is messing with you.

He ran his fingers over his forearm, feeling the flush of warmth and slight vibration of pulse beneath them.

Without thinking, he opened the window.

The cool air blew in with him, ruffling cream sheets.

What are you doing?

He had no answer.

It just feels...right.

The girl tossed, her arms reaching out into the empty space next to her, a tiny whimper escaping her lips. When her fingertips brushed the back of his hand, Cassius couldn't deny the shiver it sent through his entire being. Without thinking, he reached out for her hand, his fingers brushing the scar on her wrist.

It was like the entire world had shifted.

No, *his entire world* had shifted.

His thumb brushed the underside of her wrist, where he bit her. Where his teeth had punctured her skin and marked her blood as his.

"I don't even know your name..." he whispered.

Her fingertips grazed his forearm as he held her hand, and Cassius didn't want to let go.

"But...I promise to keep you safe." He let the words fall out in absolution. When the room had brightened with the light of dawn, only then did Cassius realize hours had passed.

The sound of footsteps in the distance alerted him.

In a flash, he leaned his body through

the window, stealing one last look at the beautiful mortal who he vowed to protect.

CHAPTER FOURTEEN

AVA STARED AT the scar. It didn't seem to want to fade.

The water ran over her skin, cleansing like rain. Ava squeezed the remnants of her body wash onto a loofah, the smell of bergamot and jasmine filling the air.

The hot water ran in rivulets down her skin, grazing over still tender wounds.

The knife wounds on her thighs were still pink in color, even after two weeks, while the bite mark on her wrist looked as if it'd been part of her skin for years.

How strange, Ava thought as she stared at the raised mark. In the beam of sunlight from the bathroom window, she noticed it shimmered.

The memory of those razor-sharp fangs pushed to the surface, and Ava's breath hitched.

The feel of his warm tongue on her flesh, like it was sealing the wound.

Ava did her best to shake the memory from her mind, and finished her shower, all too eager to leave.

The nightmare had faded into memory as she slept, as fear and pain gave way to bliss and serenity.

The feeling of wanting his touch...the

angel from the darkness.

Ava ran her fingers through her wet hair, her reflection staring back at her.

"You're losing your damn marbles, Ava. You're just messed up about Ross. That guy was just as wasted as the rest of them." She pulled on her favorite Blue Oyster Cult shirt.

"Leaving in five," Mal shouted from the hallway. The scent of percolating bold coffee struck her, and her blood chilled. Becky was up.

Fuck.

Ava hurriedly jumped into a pair of jeans, wracked with frays and holes. She grabbed her tote bag and took a deep breath as she opened her door.

When she came into the kitchen, Becky stood there in her fluffy mauve robe, with her unicorn slippers.

Despite being almost sixty-five, her aunt didn't look a day over fifty. Age had been *very* good to her.

"Good morning, Ava." Becky smiled at her with a warm smile.

Ava avoided her gaze. "Good morning," she said as she walked past the countertop where Becky and Mal sat.

"Malcolm tells me you two will be staying here for a while, what with all the hoopla up at the college." Becky sipped her coffee, and Ava pursed her lips.

Hoopla. She called the murders, hoopla.

"Yeah, well it wasn't my idea." Ava glared at Mal.

"Well, I'm glad to have you both." Becky smiled at Mal.

"Yeah, well I'm going to be late,

soooo…" She cleared her throat, her gaze fixed on her brother.

Mal pushed off the counter, his dark brown hair hanging in his eyes as he shook it away.

"On that note, we'll see you later, Becky." Mal saluted her, and Ava all but ran out the door.

Her skin prickled with goosebumps, despite the sun. She ran her hands up her arms as she opened the car.

"You cold?" Mal asked as he got in the driver side.

"Yeah, just a chill." She answered.

Mal reached in the back seat, grasping a blue flannel shirt. He handed it to Ava, who looked at it suspiciously.

"When is the last time you washed that?" She gingerly took the shirt and held it up to her nose. It didn't smell bad. It smelled like tobacco and whiskey, which wasn't an unwelcome smell.

It smelled like Mal.

"Its new. Dallas gave it to me." Mal started the car.

"Aww, how cute. You two are sharing clothes now." Ava fluttered her eyelashes at her brother in a teasing manner.

"It's not like that, and you know it." He shot her a disapproving glare as he pulled the Chevelle out of the driveway.

Ava pulled the flannel on, and she had to admit it was rather cozy.

"Where is your partner in crime, anyway? Aren't you two usually joined at the hip?" she asked as she pulled the warm flannel around her. It was a tad large for her, being that Dallas was much larger than her. Mal wasn't short by any means, but Dallas was a former wide receiver back in his high school days, and Mal...

Although Mal seemed to have put on more muscle in the last few years, she was certain he'd never stand a match with Dallas if it ever came to it.

"He's just hanging out with some friends. Said he'd meet up with us later." Mal's eyes were serious, but his tone light. "What time are you done with your classes today?" Something about the way he asked, felt...off.

Ever since the pizza shop, he's been weird.

"My last class finishes up at two," she answered.

"Cool. Listen, I've got some errands to run, so if I'm not there immediately at two..."

Ava didn't let him finish. "I'm a big

girl, Mal. I can take care of myself. It's fine. Just give me a call or something when you're close." She yawned.

"Should have gotten up earlier, maybe you could have had a cup of coffee." Mal irked her.

"I just had a rough night. I'm fine," she said as she leaned her chin on her flannel covered arm, gazing out the window at the expanse of the trees, the touch of golden autumn among them.

***

Ember pushed the paper cup toward Ava. "You really don't have to do this, you know."

Ava graciously wrapped her hands around the flimsy cup, letting its warmth seep into her skin. "I know. But I like to."

Ember smiled sweetly, her green eyes lighting up with joy.

Ava didn't know what to say. She was never good at this sort of thing.

"Thanks," she said as she took a sip of the mocha flavored coffee.

Ember took her apron off, and hung it on the uniform rack as she punched out from the cafe.

Ava leaned against the cold subway tiles as she waited for Ember to gather her things.

That's when she saw him.

The green-eyed angel from the shadows.

He stood across the room, frozen like an animal who'd been caught in the headlights.

He wore dark black pants, and a grey tee, and even from across the room, Ava could swear his green eyes, *glowed.*

The memory of his lips on her skin...

Of fangs...

Ava clutched her coffee cup.

"Ember I'll be right back," she said as normally as she could.

"Okay..." Ember's voice was faint behind her as Ava walked hastily through the crowd of students.

Why is he following me?

What is his deal?

When a student pushing a cart full of stock cut her off in the middle of her path, Ava cursed.

"Watch where you're going!" the student snapped.

Ava looked up, and the angel had once again disappeared.

About to give up, she saw the flash of golden-blond hair as he walked out the door.

Ava quickened her pace, her legs striding with purpose.

She was only a few feet away.

"Hey!" she hollered. The man ignored her.

She sprinted, the coffee sloshing with animated movement. She reached out for his arm and pulled it. The man spun around in shock. He seemed to be speechless.

"Why are you following me?" She stood on the corner of the sidewalk, casting a glare at him.

"I beg your pardon." He cleared his throat.

"You fucking bit me." She sipped her coffee.

"I...yes. I did." His answer was not cold, or remorseful.

"What the hell?" She pushed him.

He stumbled back.

"Please tell me you don't have anything." She could feel a sense of worry overcome her.

"I...no. I'm...sorry?" he asked as if he wasn't sure what to say.

"Stop following me." She said it with authority. Goosebumps prickled on her arm, inside the flannel.

"I..." He paused, and the look in his eyes was...

Ava wasn't sure how to describe it.

"I wanted to apologize." He cleared his throat, and Ava found herself staring at his mouth.

The memory of his lips on her skin...

Made her stomach flip.

She broke his gaze and took a sip of her coffee.

"Well, consider it done." She refused to look at him, but...

Something about those eyes pulled her in.

"I'm Cassius." His voice truly was like chocolate cake.

Ava glanced up at him for a fraction of a moment.

"Ava." She took a sip of her coffee.

"I'm sorry, *Ava,* if I alarmed you. I didn't mean to." The man named Cassius stood with perfect posture.

"Yeah, well I suppose we're all on edge, after what's been going on around here." She nonchalantly flipped her long dark hair over her shoulder, crossing her left arm in front of her stomach, as she tightened her grip of her right hand on the coffee cup.

"Of course." He blinked, and Ava

noticed his eyelashes were dark, and thick.

No wonder she thought he was an angel. His features were...masculine yet, *beautiful.*

Like a freaking Calvin Klein model.

"See you around, *Cas.*" She took another sip of her coffee and turned back to the union, leaving the man named Cassius in her wake.

CHAPTER FIFTEEN

CASSIUS WATCHED AS *Ava* walked away. He still couldn't' believe she'd caught up to him. When the stalker cut her off...

He thought he'd escaped unseen. But her pulse was louder, and louder with every step until...

She *touched* him. The sensation left the tiniest prickle on his skin.

And she cursed at him. And *pushed*

him.

A light smile tugged at the corner of his lips. The memory of a girl who tried with all her might to move, despite a loss of blood.

A fighter.

It wasn't as if she knew *what* he was. If she had, she certainly would not have pushed him. No, if she knew what he was...

She'd run screaming.

As she should, he reminded himself.

She'd rendered him speechless, for the first time in years.

Of course, she didn't understand what had transpired. How could she? She was just an average girl, who had no inkling about the world that lay in the shadows. Of course, to her it must have seemed like he was under the influence of alcohol or drugs. No sane *human* bit another human.

Cassius didn't know what to say, but he knew if he said nothing...she'd leave.

I need to know her name, the pressing thought assaulted him.

"I am Cassius." The words came out differently than he'd meant them.

Ava. Her name was *Ava.*

Simple, beautiful.

Cassius shook his head as he hid in the rafters, trying to ward off his burgeoning curiosity.

When the sound of the doors opening broke the silence, Cassius leaned over the rafters, peering down below.

"I'm thirsty, damn it. How much longer do you expect me to wait?" Cassius didn't recognize the voice.

"We've got to wait, a few more days at

most." A familiar head of hair came into his vision, and Cassius recognized its owner immediately.

Liam.

"It's been two weeks." A third voice chimed in. Cassius stayed as still as a statue.

"Yeah, and you can thank Brody for that. I told you to dispose of the bodies. You got sloppy, and now we have to fucking starve," Liam snarled at the one wearing a backward hat.

"I think I saw a hunter today. Red Chevelle. Guy didn't look like one of the locals," the man wearing a green golf shirt and khakis growled back at Brody.

"So now you're going to blame me for the hunters too, is that it, Logan?" Brody cornered the other vamp, his chest puffing out like a peacock puffs its feathers.

Liam snarled, challenging the other vampires. "Silence! You fools." Cassius watched as Liam entered their space, the other two vampires taking a step back.

Brody snapped his fangs at Liam. "I'm not the only one with loose ends." Brody glared at Liam.

"Liam managed to let one get away..." Brody hissed.

"The girl from Alpha Pi?" Logan asked.

"Yes. Someone marked her. I could smell his scent, mixed with her blood." Brody crossed his arms.

"She's nothing to worry about." Liam shrugged.

Cassius gripped the beam next to him tightly.

"What if she remembers... She saw

our faces. We were with her and the guy half the night." Logan sounded panicked.

"I don't think she remembers." Liam walked away from them.

"But you're not certain," Brody sneered.

"Are you going to do something about it or am I going to have to clean up your mess again?" Brody stood still, his gaze directed at Liam.

"She's marked, now. That changes things." Liam's voice was solid.

"Well, I've never been afraid of a challenge." Brody smiled.

Liam was in front of Brody within a flash, his fingers poised around Brody's thick neck. Liam bared his fangs. "She's mine to savor, and you best remember your rank." The authority in Liam's voice was direct.

Brody's body shook, his gaze never leaving Liam.

When Liam let him go, Cassius couldn't stand to stay. He crawled through the rooftop latch, and jumped into the shadows of abandoned construction, with one sole purpose.

CHAPTER SIXTEEN

AVA SAT CROSS-LEGGED on the bench, peering down at her textbook, a steaming cup of hot chocolate held close to her chest. The sweet wisps of steam filled her senses with warmth and comfort.

When black boots came into her vision, Ava looked up.

The man who stood before her wore dark wash jeans, his black leather belt boasting a rather ostentatious buckle that looked like a pentagram. Ava let her gaze travel up from his waist to see he was wearing a black muscle tank, his black tribal tattoos standing out against his defined muscles.

She'd know those tattoos anywhere.

"You look good in my shirt there, kitten." His voice was deep with bravado, tinged with sarcasm.

Ava's eyes lit up as she stared back into his pale blue eyes. Bright like the crest of a tsunami.

His dark hair was cut short, shorter than the last time she'd seen him, and he looked like he hadn't shaved in a few days. When her brother tried to pull off the grungy look, he failed miserably, but on Jake Dallas the look added to his charm.

"I believe it's Mal's shirt now." She let her eyes fall back to the book in her lap.

Dallas shifted his weight.

"Mal's running a bit late. So, it looks like I'm your ride." Dallas jiggled a set of keys in front of her.

Ava sat up straighter.

"Where'd you park?" She closed her book and set her hot chocolate down to pack up her tote bag.

Dallas nodded over to the library. "Over by the cafe."

Ava all but leaped off the bench.

She had always been slightly taller than most people, but up against Dallas she felt short.

"Please. tell me you brought the bike." She could feel a smile forming on her lips.

Dallas smiled, the motion reaching

his eyes. "Just for you, kitten." He winked at her.

Ava smiled. "Sweet," she said excitedly as she followed him to the library.

Despite the thirteen-year age gap between them, Ava had to admit Dallas looked like he fit in perfectly with the rest of the young students at Chester U, despite being in his thirties.

Probably could wipe out half the football team too.

She noticed quite a few of the students gawking at him as they strode over to his motorcycle.

When Ava climbed on the back of his motorcycle and wrapped her arms around his tree trunk of a waist, she couldn't help but smile.

***

Ava released her hands from Dallas's waist, and took off her helmet, tousling her long, dark hair free. The wind blew long strands in her face, and Dallas let out a small laugh.

"What?" Ava said as she pulled the strands from her face.

"You look like a damn shampoo commercial." Dallas hung his helmet on the handlebar.

"I'll take that as a compliment," she said as she walked past him to the front door. She didn't wait for him to come inside.

"Hello, Ava." Becky sat on the couch with a glass of wine, and the sound made Ava jump only slightly.

"And...Jake? How lovely to see you again." She smiled at him and took a sip of her wine.

Ava felt uncomfortable at the gaze she shot in Dallas's direction.

Dallas nodded to her. "Evening, Miss Michaels," he said politely.

Ava brushed past the kitchen counter, where Connie milled about. It looked as if she was baking something. Ava peered over her shoulder. *Cookies.* Ava reached her hand around Connie, only to be met with Chinese curses and a smack on the hand.

"Don't even think about it," Connie said nonchalantly.

"But I'm hungry," Ava whined.

"You're always hungry, child. It's a wonder you're as skinny as a rail." Connie smiled as she finished icing a cookie. She turned to Ava and held it out to her, her eyebrow raised.

Ava took it gingerly from her hands. "Thank you, Connie." She smiled and graciously took a bite of the cookie.

It tasted like almonds and sweet vanilla. Ava opened the door and walked out on to the patio.

Dallas wasn't far behind her.

"Don't tell me I have to help you with your homework too," he said as he plopped down in one of the Adirondack chairs, letting his legs sprawl out. Leaning up against the chair back, the motion made him look rather enticing.

Ava shot him a glance.

"You wouldn't be much help anyway. I doubt you know anything about the Middle Ages," she said as she took another bite of her cookie and sat down in one of the rockers.

"I know they were big into the occult.

Lots of interesting lore and myths."

"Fascinating. Jake Dallas knows something," she teased.

"I know a lot of things, Ava." He raised his eyebrow at her.

"I bet you do." She finished her cookie.

"Ava don't take this the wrong way..." Dallas leaned forward.

"What's up?" She noted the change in his demeanor.

"Mal told me about what happened to your friend. Up on campus—the one from the news." Dallas looked slightly uncomfortable.

"You're not going to lecture me about staying in and being a good girl too, are you?" Ava raised her eyebrow, her frustration evident.

"No. I'm not." He paused, brushing

his hands together.

Ava sighed, crossing her arms. "Then, what is it?"

"Have you ever taken...like...a self-defense class?" The way Dallas phrased the question felt odd.

"You mean like, how to fend off a rapist?" Ava shot him a pointed look.

"Umm...yeah," Dallas looked a bit nervous.

"Not really, but..." she started to speak, and Dallas rose from his seat.

"Get up." He motioned for her to get up.

"Wha..." she said as she pushed herself up out of the chair.

Dallas walked over to the grassy expanse of the backyard.

"Come at me." He motioned for her, planting his feet firmly on the ground.

"Dallas, no. Seriously..." She crossed her arms.

"Come on." His eyes challenged her.

"This is stupid," she bit out.

"Humor me, kitten." The look in his eyes was dark, and challenging.

"Fine," she said as she approached him, and without warning, threw the hardest punch she'd ever thrown, directly into his jaw.

Dallas looked slightly shocked, but retaliated, nonetheless.

"Is that all you've got?" He said as he withdrew his fingers from his bloodied lip, a smile forming on his face.

***

She was sweating, and so was he, and it felt *good.* Even though there were no stakes, and she knew Dallas would not harm her, he didn't hold back. Ava had to admit it felt *good* to spar. She'd never considered herself an athlete by any means, not like Dallas was. She'd stuck out cheerleading until she graduated, not because she loved the hustle and bustle of high school football, but because there was something about being thrown into the air, about the training that she really liked. She'd also really enjoyed her kickboxing class over the summer.

Dallas wrapped his arms around her, his hold tight, fingers tightening around her wrist. She backed herself into his hold, angling her elbow, but the touch of his fingers on her wrist *stung* as they grazed her bite. He stilled, and Ava could hear his sharp intake of breath. The fun, laughing tone he'd had disappeared as he pulled her wrist to him.

"How the hell did you get this?" His voice darkened, his thumb brushing the cool mark on her skin.

Ava breathed deep, caught between answering him, and taking advantage of his distraction. She settled on the latter because she wasn't sure *what* to say.

"What the hell is going on out here?" Becky's voice was alarmed and Mal's curses accentuated the air.

Dallas held Ava's arms tightly in front of her, and his body pressed against hers like a brick wall.

Ava wriggled once more, positioning her elbow directly into his groin.

Dallas, distracted once more by the presence of Mal and Becky, was at her mercy. He breathed in a huff of air as she applied the force and stepped on his foot with her free hand, breaking free. He looked at her curiously, but only for a moment, as his natural demeanor returned, leaving that unanswered question in the air.

"Just an old-fashioned sparring session." Dallas chuckled.

"Dallas thought he'd show me some self-defense moves." Ava brushed her hair behind her.

"What a nice idea. Perhaps you could share some of that knowledge with me, Jake?" Becky said.

Ava felt her stomach twitch, and a strange prickling sensation arose on her skin. Her wrist flared beneath Dallas's flannel, the heat trapped with nowhere to go as she pulled it tight against her wrist, the faint sting from where he'd touched her still present.

The feeling washed over her, and the memories pushed forth to the surface.

Ross carried her, rather unsteadily. She wrapped her legs around his waist, uncontrollable giggles eliciting from her throat.

When Ross fell, she collapsed on top of him, the laughter a full on roar.

"Shh... Ava..." Ross's whisper was less of a whisper and more of a loud beacon.

She rolled off him, trying to catch her breath.

"You are shit faced." She turned her head, her eyes fixated on his bleary, heavy-lidded eyes.

"Oh, like you're not..." He shoved at her, the smile on his face genuine.

Ava leaned up on her elbows, the bottom of her dress riding up her thighs.

The floor was cold and wet.

A figure emerged from the darkness behind Ross, but she couldn't make out the face.

He seemed to be wearing a blue checkered shirt.

Ava shook the memory off and noticed Mal was staring at her.

"What's your deal?" she said as she brushed past him toward the living room.

"I don't know what you're talking about." Mal looked at her with question.

Ava watched as Connie made arrangements to the last of the dinner plates on the island in the kitchen.

"You've been weird ever since yesterday." She crossed her arms.

"Maybe I think you're the one being weird." Mal twisted his lips.

"Whatever. You want to be all shadows and secrets, be my guest." She walked into the kitchen and took sight of Connie's dinner. Her heart lifted a fraction at the realization Connie made her favorite cheesy potatoes.

The sound of the door opening broke her concentration.

"Leaving so soon, Jake?" Becky called

"I'm afraid so. I uh...promised to meet up with some friends while I was in town." He smiled lightly.

Mal turned in his direction. "Thanks, Dallas." His voice was serious.

Dallas smirked, and saluted Mal. "Don't mention it."

In the blink of an eye, he was gone.

Becky sat in her usual spot at the dining table, Connie pulling up next to her. Mal stocked his plate full of cheesy potatoes and chicken, leaving out all the other sides, before sitting down.

Ava reluctantly filled her plate and sat next to her brother.

"Isn't this nice, the four of us together again." Becky smiled.

Ava focused on her chicken.

"How long are you in town, Malcolm?" Connie asked.

Ava looked at her brother, waiting for his answer.

"A few weeks." He took a bite of cheesy potatoes.

A few weeks?

Ava couldn't remember the last time Mal had stayed longer than a week.

"I'm so glad you decided to come home for a bit as dwell, Ava. I can't imagine how terrifying it must be, what with a serial killer preying on the campus grounds."

Ava focused on her food.

"I tell you, I feel so much better knowing you are safe under my roof. And how nice of Dallas to help you feel confident about defending yourself." She took a sip of her wine.

"I don't need Dallas to tell me how to take care of myself." Ava chewed her chicken furiously.

"Of course, you don't. But you can always learn new tricks." Mal spoke seriously.

"I'm the one who gave him a bloody lip." Ava cast a glare at Mal.

She could still feel the flush of heat at her wrist, and a wave of nausea overcame her.

Ava was so tired, and the room was spinning.

Ross was in the corner with one of the fraternity brothers. The one who'd been making eyes at him all evening. Ava was only slightly surprised Ross wasn't offended.

The man had his mouth on Ross's neck.

Ava could feel cold, clammy hands at her shoulder, pulling her away.

"Don't touch me..." She tried to twist out of their grasp, but her legs wouldn't move.

Ross moaned in pleasure, and Ava's eyes felt heavy.

She could feel slick hands sliding up her legs. She tried to shift away, but...

Why couldn't' she move?

"Ross...." She tried to form words, but...

Ross moaned in pleasure, and Ava felt

a sharp pain from inside her thigh...

She let out a whimper as she tore her head from Ross's gaze.

She was bleeding...

Another prickle of pain sent a shockwave through her body, and she could see one of the brothers, the one with the backward hat...

Between her legs.

She forced the numb, deadweight legs with all her might, into his head. The motion knocked him over, and Ava felt exhausted, as her thigh wounds throbbed.

The man pulled his fingers away from his lips, and she noted the blood on his lip. It looked...black.

"Bitch. Just for that I ought to give you another one." He snarled, and Ava could see his teeth looked...odd.

Sharp.

The feel of the knife cutting into her skin was quick, but not without pain.

She attempted to move her leg, but it was like it didn't belong to her. It was heavy, and it hurt.

Ava's stomach felt queasy, and the scent of blood and mildew filled her senses.

Ava pushed herself away from the table abruptly. "Excuse me," she said as politely as possible, trying to hold in her emotion.

"Ava..." Becky started.

"I'm just going to the bathroom. Chill." Ava knew her voice was harsh, much more than she intended. She shut the door quickly, bracing her hands on the cold marble of the sink.

BLOOD & BONES

CHAPTER SEVENTEEN

IT WAS A strange feeling for Cassius, the pulsing radar in his veins. Despite growing up in the center of vampiric history, with Leon and Cora, his parents, and even Eden and Octavius, he didn't know much about the claiming of human blood. Leon's studies in the 1980's fared more toward the effect of fresh blood alternatives than they did on the blood of those marked.

Though Cassius knew his father marked his mother first before turning her, he hadn't thought to press his father for information on the matter. He was far too angry at the man for leaving him in the dust because he'd thought Cassius didn't belong to him.

Because he hadn't made his transformation fast enough.

Not to mention, Cassius's blood haze left him longing for one thing, and one thing only.

He'd tried to keep his human friendships at a distance, and romance of any sort was out of the questions. Until Eden, that was, but she was not human. She was a monster. Like him.

He wondered momentarily as he walked past the gates of Ava's residence, how his father could stand such a bright, noticeable feeling in his blood for seven years.

Cassius could barely stand it now, and it had only been mere weeks.

The fading sunset cast a golden glow over the plantation house, and Cassius couldn't help but remember a similar sunset, over the Duquensian Manor only a carriage ride away from Portofino.

Thoughts of *her* crept into his mind, souring the memory.

She'd been a different person then, Eden. She'd been mysterious, alluring, and unlike any other woman he'd met in his short twenty-four years of life. She'd been caring. A friend. She'd taken him under her dark wings.

Before he could move, the front door swung open, and Ava ran down the steps, flinging herself through the gates, and smacked into him.

He held his hands out to steady, her, the feel of his fingers on her skin sending tiny flashes of warmth through him.

"Ava?" he asked as she looked up at him, confusion in her eyes. She pushed away from his light touch, and he noticed the drop in temperature from her departure.

"What the fuck, Cas? Are you fucking *stalking* me...still?" Her eyes flashed with anger.

His gaze dropped to her wrist, and he could *feel* her blood racing as if it were his own.

I am absolutely not stalking you. I just...

His brain wanted to protest. After all, he'd only sought to walk among the main streets, to clear his mind.

He'd given in to the pull of her pulse, followed it to the gates of her estate.

It wasn't *not* stalking.

A sense of shame fell over him.

This isn't me. He thought. But as soon as the thought crossed his mind, so did the memory of Liam, Brody, and Logan discussing their 'loose ends'.

She needs to know the truth. But how do I tell her? Surely, she will cast me off as insane, and why shouldn't she?

"I did not know you resided here," he lied. A small pang of guilt shot through him at the action.

He'd told many lies in his long life, so why was this one different?

Why did he feel the need to tell this mortal everything?

Ava narrowed her eyes at him

skeptically. "Why do I not believe you?" She took off down the sidewalk.

"Where are you going?" he asked curiously.

Her long dark hair blew in the rustle of wind, and tiny autumn leaves followed in her dust.

"What kind of idiot do you take me for? Why would I tell you anything? You're the one stalking me, remember?"

Cassius was at her side immediately. "Perhaps, we could talk?" He tried to sound as polite and safe as possible.

Ava glanced at him once more, but she didn't run. She kept up with his pace.

"You have until I reach my destination to plead your case." She smirked, and Cassius noted she seemed to slow down only a fraction.

"About the other night..." He opened his mouth and Ava only rolled her eyes.

"What about it?" They turned the corner block, passing Cory's. The neon flashed, casting an aqua and red glow on her features.

"I bit you." Cassius found strangely enough the words came easily, though he was certain after he told her the truth, she'd probably run.

Far away from him.

A part of him regretted the truth that would undoubtedly separate her from him.

This close to her, he could smell the hint of jasmine, feel her pulse within him like a steady, flowing river.

He followed her stride down the street, passing the tiny accountant office, and homes.

"Yeah, and now I'll have your fucking teeth marks on my wrist forever. That shit left a scar, you know,"

I can work with this.

"I'm not...like you." He struggled to speak the words, knowing the destruction they were about to bring.

Ava stopped, in front of the library and turned to him, causing him to abruptly stop himself.

"Really now? What are you going to tell me you're a vampire or something?" She raised her eyebrows at him, and her tone was sarcastic.

Cassius felt awash with heat that had nothing to do with pulse, nothing to do the weather. It seemed like forever until he found the words.

"Actually, yes. I am. A vampire. It is my venom that healed your wounds." He stood straight, his eyes never breaking her gaze.

Ava rolled her eyes and laughed.

"Fucking delusional too. You're a piece of work, aren't you, Cassius? God damn, it's always the fucking hot ones that are completely bonkers." She turned away from him, as if to move forward and leave him as he deserved, but instead she remained in place. She turned her head once more, in his direction.

Did she just call me...hot? Cassius wasn't sure how to take her words. They were spoken with sarcasm, after all.

"A fucking vampire? Like Dracula-I-want-to-suck-your-blood-vampire?" Her lips twisted in a sarcastic smile, but he could see her eyes betrayed her. And even if they hadn't, the increased pulse inside of him told him she considered the truth in his words.

"Yes. Although, I don't particularly care for that comparison. Most of the stories have it all wrong." He swallowed nervously, his hands finding their way into his pockets.

Ava stood still, facing the dusk.

"Those men...the ones that attacked your friend..."

Ava turned around slowly, her amber eyes tinged with alarm.

"They were vampires too. The girls at The Heights..." The words poured out of him without warning now, faster and faster. The overwhelming feeling of caring, the swell of protectiveness he felt toward this girl, this *Ava*, was startling to him, but he also had to admit that it wasn't entirely the mark's fault. He'd cared for humans before. Friends like Penny, Rocco, Marguerite, Pierre. He'd felt protective of them too, once, without a mark to blame.

You always have to be the hero, don't you? Eden's words swam in his head.

"You're telling me, that the murders plaguing Chester are because of *vampires*?" She chewed at her lip.

"I know it sounds crazy..." The golden sunset lit her up from behind like a halo.

"You're absolutely right. It *is* crazy." Her voice was even as she looked up at him.

"But you know it is true...don't you?" He refused to move from his spot, noting the space between them.

Ava stalked closer to him, her eyes burning with fire.

With her pulse racing beneath his

skin, he could tell she was frightened. The last thing he wanted was to frighten her, but—

"Your time is up. If I catch you *stalking* me again, vampire or not, I will make your life a living hell, Cassius. You will regret the day you fucking bit me. Am I clear?" Her eyes burned into his, and he nodded in response.

"Absolutely."

CHAPTER EIGHTEEN

VAMPIRE.

The word reverberated in her cerebellum, and although she knew she should run, far away from this crazy stalker, her wrist burned with heat, her skin prickled with goosebumps, and as she looked into glowing green eyes, she knew it was true.

She knew it in her blood.

She lay in her bed, her gaze settled

on the shimmering scar on her wrist. In his presence it burned, while the rest of her skin felt tiny prickles of ice, goosebumps. It was insane to think *he* had something to do with it, but she knew. She'd always been a believer in the paranormal; after all, it was in her blood. She'd known the lengths her family went to, changing their names to Michaels, because they wanted to escape the shadow of their family's lineage. Crowley.

Ava had always felt drawn to her history, being a descendant of one of the most famous occultists in history. She'd amassed a small collection of books on such things—witchcraft, ghosts, divination, cryptozoology. But vampires—

She tossed in her bed, turning over

on her stomach, looking out the window at the dark forest beyond.

If what Cassius said was true...that vampires truly were the ones responsible for the murders at Chester...responsible for Ross's death...

How do I fight off something that isn't even human?

Ava could throw a punch, and even evade an attacker, but a vampire? She doubted a solid right hook would deter something with fangs and super strength that wasn't alive or dead.

A knock sounded on her door, and Ava jumped.

Mal stood in the doorway.

"Hey, Simba." His voice was serious, and in the harsh shadows of the hallway, she could see the highlight of the hallway lights on his face. Mal hadn't looked this serious since their parent's funeral.

"Can I come in?" he asked, and she didn't miss the worry in his voice.

"Of course." She nodded and he entered, shutting the door behind him.

"There's something we need to talk about. I know you're going to have a lot of questions...but..." Mal ran his hand through his hair as he took a seat in the butterfly chair in front of her desk. He leaned on his knees, running his hands over his face before continuing.

"Mal is everything ok..."

"Dallas told me you've been bit."

Memories of earlier, of her spar with Dallas flashed in her mind.

His fingers running over her skin, brushing her bite mark on her wrist. The sting.

Cassius's...vampire bite.

Of course, she thought.

He must have seen it and wondered what happened. Any sane person would wonder why one had teeth mark scars on their wrist.

"It's nothing, just... I was at a party and things got...out of hand."

She hid her wrist under her pillow.

"I haven't told you the truth. I thought...I thought I could keep it from you. That'd you'd be safer if you didn't know but...clearly I was wrong."

Mal looked into her eyes, and she could see sadness and fear in them.

"Mal, you're not making sense." She hugged her pillow in front of her.

"All the trips I go on, Ava.... I'm not *just* playing gigs."

Ava's blood chilled. It was as if she

knew what was coming, and she didn't want to hear it any more than Mal wanted to speak it.

"I hunt monsters, Ava. The kind that bite you...and leave marks like the one on your wrist. The kind that makes the monster under the bed look tame. The kind..."

"Vampires, you mean." Her fingers tightened around the pillow, squeezing it with anxious energy.

"Yes. Dallas too. He's my partner. We hunt them together."

Ava blinked her eyes, trying to hold back the onslaught of emotion that seemed to be trying to push its way up and out of her through her eyes.

"Vampires aren't real..." she whispered. But even as she said it, she knew it was not true.

"Unfortunately, Ava they are very real. And you've been bitten by one."

CHAPTER NINETEEN

AVA TRIED TO focus on the lecture, but she couldn't. Not that she didn't find Medieval history interesting, she'd always loved *history*, but the slides of classical paintings amidst the dark lecture hall made it easy to zone out.

That, and she couldn't stop thinking about Cassius.

Every ounce of her being *knew* he was telling the truth, and if she'd had any qualms about it, Mal's visit squashed any doubt.

That explains the dusty amp.

Ava glanced around the spacious lecture hall, her gaze settling on the various heads in the chairs, and she couldn't help but wonder if one of them was next, or if one of them was not who they seemed.

Ava's skin prickled with goosebumps, and her wrist flared with heat as three men ambled down the steps in the darkness, and she couldn't deny her curiosity as she turned.

Liam and his friends sauntered down the steps, quietly, and as they passed her, Liam shot her a devilish smirk. "Ava." He smiled lightly as he passed her.

His friend, the one who'd irritated Mal

at the pizza shop, gave her a sly grin as he passed, and flashes of memories pushed forth.

Brody.

Dark eyes peering up at her from between her legs, black blood on his lips.

That backward hat.

Ava felt her blood chill as she watched them travel the steps to the seats in the front of the room, taking the prickle of ice and heated sensation with them.

Well, that can't be coincidence.

"Do you know those guys?" Ember whispered, poking her arm.

Ava turned to her friend. "I think so," she answered.

Ember's brows furrowed together. "What do you mean you *think* so?" she pushed.

"They were at the party. You know, the one I went to with Ross." Ava slumped in her seat, her head rolling back on the padded backing of the chair. The slide changed, the bright lights in the darkness showing another classical painting.

"Are you going to the service?" Ember asked.

Ava shifted uncomfortably in her seat. Without any leads, and no physical evidence, it wasn't likely Ross's body would be found. They'd declared him deceased, if only for the closure it would provide his family. The funeral service at St. Sebastian's Church was in three days. It was televised everywhere, posters strewn all throughout the bulletin boards and message boards on campus, and she hadn't been able to look at any of them.

The reality of his death was everywhere.

It haunted her every move, and even more so now that she knew the truth behind his demise.

Fucking vampires. Truth is always stranger than fiction.

"I don't know." It was an honest answer.

Ember pursed her lips, her hand still on Ava's arm. Warm, friendly, soothing.

"Well, if you decide you want to go, you don't have to go alone." She smiled sweetly.

"Thanks."

The lights came on, and Ava glanced at her phone.

2:00.

The sound of bristling students

shoving books and binders into bags and backpacks echoed in the hall. Ember slung her backpack over her shoulder as she scooted past Ava to the hallway to join the crowd.

"See you tomorrow." She smiled as she faded out between the stream of students in a hurry for their next class.

When the crowd diminished, Ava exited out of the building as well. When she stepped out of the shade of the building, her lips twisted into a smile. Dallas leaned against his motorcycle, and the bright sunlight shone down on him, casting shadows on his thick arms, his tattoos standing out vividly even at a distance from his sleeveless muscle shirt.

"Would it kill you to wear a shirt that didn't have gaping holes in it?" She stopped in front of him, watching him spin his keys amidst his thick fingers. His blue eyes sparkled with charm.

"You know what they say, flaunt it if you got it." He smirked.

Ava rolled her eyes. "Too bad you're old. I hear things stop working after you turn thirty." She grabbed the helmet he offered her.

"Oh, I can assure you, kitten, my machine is in perfect working order." He winked as he straddled his bike, the motion elongating his thighs, strained against his dark wash jeans.

"Where's Mal?" she asked as she positioned herself behind him.

"He had some business to take care of. He'll meet up with us later."

Ava wrapped her arms around Dallas's waist, her fingers brushing against his abs through his flimsy tank. They felt hard and warm.

"You know, I could get used to this mode of transportation. It's pretty badass." She held on tight to him.

Dallas turned his head slightly, regarding her with a smile.

"I'll show you badass. Hang tight, kitten."

***

"What the hell is this?" Ava dismounted off the bike, staring at the unassuming building buried in the brick wall in front of her. It didn't look like anything....operable.

"Mal told me he had the talk with you." Dallas hung the helmet on the handlebar, kicking down the kickstand to rest on the side of the broken concrete walk.

It was hard to believe anyone even knew about the place, being as it was far out, and not surrounded by much more than an abandoned gas station, and a half-crumbled structure.

"That doesn't explain why you brought me to this hole in the wall." She cast him a rueful glance.

"Is this your idea of badass? Because if it is, I think we need to have a serious talk. Your dementia may be setting in." She jabbed him.

"Come on." He motioned for her to follow, and she did.

Ava had seen plenty of gyms, both in her cheerleading days in Massachusetts, and in her time in Chester, but she'd never seen a gym like this.

Despite being embedded into a hobbit

hole, the place was pristine and well kept. It didn't boast traditional machines, although there were a few she recognized. Leg lifts, barbell benches, push up machines. There was a boxing ring, as well as a track that looked like the paint was fresh.

"What the hell is this place?" She turned to Dallas once more.

"Self-defense is a little different with supernatural forces." His voice was serious.

"Dallas..." she started.

"I know it's a lot to take in, okay? I've been there. Trust me." He licked his lips, and Ava couldn't deny the motion sent a shiver directly to her groin.

Fuck me.

She'd known Dallas as Mal's best friend for the last three years, and though he was *much* older than her, she couldn't deny that she found him insanely attractive.

At least on the outside.

She knew him fairly well, and knew enough that like Mal, Dallas wasn't really the kind of man you brought home to your parents.

Like Mal, he was the kind of guy you *hid* from your parents. Ross may have been out of her league, but at least he was in the ballpark.

Dallas was definitely out of the ballpark. He was out of the fucking state.

"I suppose next you're going to tell me the tooth fairy is real," she drawled as she dropped her backpack on the floor. She ran her hands along the ropes of the boxing ring.

"Not quite, but the whole teeth thing has some merit. Offering your bones for blessings is pretty much witchy shit 101. Right along with blowing out candles on your birthday."

She turned to see him in the boxing ring, his hand outstretched to hers.

"You up for a round two, kitten?" His eyes settled on hers, and she couldn't help but smirk.

"What, are you going to pretend to be a big bad vampire and come after me?" She set her hand in his and let him pull her up.

"Something like that."

She stepped on the soft floor of the ring and watched Dallas take his stance.

"First thing you need to know about bloodsuckers is their natural defense. Thrall."

Dallas stalked her closely, boxing her into the back of the ring post. She ducked and weaved around him, and he smiled.

"When a vampire corners you, you'll feel this…energy. Like your head gets hazy, foggy." They danced lightly, and he turned, grasping her arm behind her, pressing himself into her back, like they had the day before, when they'd been in the backyard. His other hand held her wrist across her chest, fingers brushing her scar, with that ripe sting. His lips were at her neck, and she could feel his breath heating her skin.

She closed her eyes and tried to focus. Being wrapped up like this, the weight of him against her chilled her bones, and flashes of the party reared their ugly head. That feeling of hopelessness, of terror.

The loss of control.

She struggled against Dallas, but he held her tightly.

"Thrall placates you. It makes you malleable, seeps into your brain. So, when they get close..." His lips were at her ear, and his breath on her earlobe left her stomach in knots.

"You'll likely start to feel aroused. Don't worry, that's a natural reaction. It doesn't mean you *want* them. It just means their thrall is doing what it's supposed to. Sex and blood go hand in hand for vampires."

Ava pushed back against him, trying to angle her elbow just right.

The feeling of the knife cutting into her flesh was vivid in her mind.

Of her legs knocking into Brody's

head.

Of green eyes that stared into hers.

Razor sharp fangs piercing her skin.

She'd felt hazy, blissful. Like his lips on her wrist were the most perfect thing in the world. Dallas's words juxtaposed with her memories, and she couldn't deny that as she thought about Cassius's lips on her skin, it awakened deep feelings within her.

That must be the thrall.

"How do I fight it?" she asked, her voice much breathier than she intended.

"Thrall takes hold of your mind, Ava. Not your body. That is yours." His words broke through her thoughts. "Break my hold." He directed her. "Fight me."

His voice was dark, and sultry and

Ava had to admit a part of her didn't want to. A part of her wanted to feel his pressure, wanted to relinquish, and give in to the things that filled her head. But if she couldn't fight Dallas, how would she ever fight off someone like Cassius? Death would be inevitable.

And there was no reason she could trust that even though Cassius had saved her, he wouldn't make good on his claim. She didn't know him. Not really.

He was a vampire after all. She might not have known all the finer details of a vampire's biology, but she was pretty sure they didn't save people. They killed them. There were no stories of vampires sweeping in to rescue damsels in distress. *Not that I'm a damsel. Or in distress.*

"Focus your mind. Feel your

surroundings, anticipate my moves." He gripped her wrist with his fingers around her chest, while his other hand tightened around her wrist that he held against her back. Her muscles were starting to tense.

Ava closed her eyes, and pushed past the initial shock, and arousal, and focused on the feeling of immobility, the loss of control.

Images of Brody between her legs surfaced, and she remembered the feeling of her leg's deadweight. She was on the brink of death, she knew that. Yet she'd found the will to knock her legs into his head enough to make his lip bleed. Enough to distract him.

When Ava pushed forth against Dallas, there was only one thought in her mind.

The prevailing thought was that she would be better. She would not shrink like a violet in the face of danger.

Especially if danger is tall, blond, and fucking sexy as hell.

It was as if a switch had been flipped, and as she fought her way out of his hold, and he sparred against her, she felt a burgeoning sense of urgency she hadn't had before.

"Not bad for a first shot." Dallas ran his hands through his hair before removing his shirt. He'd worked up quite a sweat. His tan skin glistened in the low light.

Ava let her cardigan fall to the ground, revealing just her Blue Oyster Cult shirt, which was starting to cling to her arms from her own sheen of sweat.

"I can work with that." He smiled as

he waved her on, challenging her once more. Ava smiled at the invitation.

CHAPTER TWENTY

"WHAT'S YOUR DEAL? You've been moping around here like a bitch for two days." Taj fell onto the couch next to Cassius. Jasmine sat in the armchair across from them with a beer in hand.

"I do not mope." Cassius scowled.

"What happened, Doc run out of your favorite veggie shake?" Taj teased.

"I told Ava the truth."

"Who's Ava?" Jasmine raised her

eyebrow.

Taj grumbled, running his hand over his face.

"Great. The pain in the ass has a name now."

"The girl from the party? "Jasmine smiled, taking a sip of her beer.

"Yeah, that's the one." Cassius leaned back into the cushions.

Her pulse still beat within his veins, but it was faint. As if she was far away.

"What do you mean you told her the truth?" Taj crossed his arms and legs. His ankle rested on his knee, and in the low light of the house, he looked every bit the bodyguard he was once was in the 80's when they'd first met.

Things were so much simpler then.

But Cassius knew he wouldn't trade the present for the past.

He'd come a long way from a scared, newborn vampire in the late 1800's. His life had been racked with blood and death since the day he was born.

He'd vowed to never be like his father; never to force a woman into this bond of blood.

Never to claim a mate.

Never to give his body and his Aurelian curse over to someone he didn't love.

And after Leon had discovered sustainable alternatives to fresh blood, he'd vowed never to drink a human again.

I may have been born a monster, but only I can control whether I am one.

"I told her what I am. What I did to her."

"Why on God's green earth would you

do that? I thought we both agreed you needed to—"

"No. I will not harm her." Cassius flashed his eyes at Taj.

"Cassius..."

"I made a vow, Taj. I know you think I'm crazy, but I value human life. I do not wish to be the end of it. I claimed her blood so that she could live another day. I know I will have to make a decision eventually. But until then, she should know the truth. Just in case-—"

"Just in case, what Cas? Just in case Liam decides to finish what he started? She's just a girl. She's nothing special, Cas. Just another fucking stray cat you can't keep." Taj's words were bold, and angry but they weren't unjust.

"Taj! That's enough." Jasmine's voice raised an octave.

Taj balled his fist.

"I'll figure it out, Taj." Cassius pushed off the sofa and walked quietly toward the back porch. It was a quiet night in the woods outside Chester. The sky was starless, and the water in the in-ground pool gleamed like black liquid, the only source of light a tiny reflection on the waves from the moon. He sat on the chaise as he reached into his pocket and pulled out a flyer.

It seemed that a funeral service was being held for the first victim, Ross Parish. Ava's...*friend.*

Boyfriend.

He remembered her words as she looked in his eyes, begging him to save not her, but her boyfriend.

It was such a selfless thing—despite the fact she was bleeding out on the concrete floor, it wasn't *her* life she asked to be spared.

It was his.

Taj was wrong. She was special.

The light in her eyes, the fight that would not leave her as she pushed with all her might to move her legs. To get up, in the face of death and prevail.

A part of him wondered if she'd be there, at the service.

Are you stalking me...still?

It wouldn't hurt to pay his respects. He wasn't like Liam or the rest of the Boracelli's. Human life mattered to him. After all, he was human once too.

The shells his kind bled and discarded had names. Lives.

Cassius folded the flyer neatly back up and set it in his pocket once more, before heading out into the darkness of night to live once more.

CHAPTER TWENTY-ONE

AVA HIT THE bottom of the boxing ring with a thump. Her blood raced, her long hair she'd pulled into a ponytail whipping around and hitting her in the face as she scrambled to an upright position.

Dallas bounced back and forth, cracking his neck.

Ava felt the adrenaline surging through her, sweat dripping down her temples, her muscles aching. Though she knew if she sat long enough, the exhaustion would truly hit her. She pushed herself up and challenged Dallas once more.

There was something about the rush of it all, that made her feel...alive.

Powerful.

Ava lunged for Dallas once more, and he captured her in his arms. Breaking his hold was easier, this time. She'd started to anticipate his movement, just as he had told her too.

She pushed against him, her fingers sliding along his sweat slicked bicep, her breathing heavy.

"Getting tired yet, kitten?" he purred in her ear.

"Fuck no," she breathed back, a smile coursing over her face.

Just as she broke free once more, the door opened, and the scent of Chinese food wafted in. Ava turned her head to see Mal carrying a couple brown paper bags, with two men she didn't recognize behind him.

"Thought I'd find you two here," Mal grumbled as he set the bags down a steel table near the door. His gaze flashed to Ava.

Ava wiped the strands of her messy hair from her face and took in the sight of the strangers. She noted they were both tall, but not quite as tall as Dallas. The man beside Mal had a mop of dark, curly black hair, and even at a distance Ava could see his eyes were silvery grey. Against his tanned skin, the contrast was quite noticeable, especially given the fact he was wearing all black. Black tee shirt, black jeans, black boots.

The other man who walked his way across the track to some cabinet over by the wall, was much less...brooding looking. Against Mal, Dallas and the lost member of a goth metal band, he looked more like a student at Chester than he did a hunter, with his bronze skin, tight-fitting black jeans, and tight-fitting flannel that was rolled up to his elbows. His stature was lean, but Ava could see the muscles in his arm as he opened the cabinet. When he turned to her, she noted his eyes were bright blue, his hair dirty blond. He kind of reminded her of Liam.

"Who's your new friend, Jake?" The dark-haired metal enthusiast asked.

Before Dallas could even answer, Mal spoke up as he opened the bags of take out, pulling out boxes and arranging them on the table.

"Vinny, Tito...meet Ava, my sister."

Tito's head whipped around, and as he did so, Ava could see in the cabinet.

It was stocked with knives and...were those *stakes*?

"You're Mal's sister?" Tito raised an eyebrow.

Ava felt a wash of anger, probably due to the adrenaline, and the surprised tone he took.

"Yeah, what of it?" She stood straight, angling her shoulders, her eyes staring down Tito. After going several rounds with Dallas, she was feeling quite a rush, and as if she could take on the world.

Tito grabbed a long knife and passed the boxing ring.

"Just expected you to be a little

less..." Tito's voice trailed off, as if he couldn't find the correct words. Perhaps he just didn't want to offend Mal.

Ava jumped down from the ring and walked up to him, her eyes fixated on his knife.

"A little less what?" She cocked her head to the side, and she could hear Dallas snickering behind her.

"Abrasive, for one." Tito raised his eyebrows.

"That's rich coming from someone who looks like he raided Justin Beiber's closet." Ava turned past him, and she could hear more laughter now.

"Hope you still like pork lo mein, Simba." Mal slid a carton of steaming food in her direction.

"Thanks." She took the carton and a package of chopsticks before sitting on the seat in one of the leg lifts.

"Where's Hunter?" Dallas jumped down from the ring as well and wiped at the sweat on his face and chest with his crumpled-up muscle tank. His thick hands running the fabric over his chest was not a bad view.

Ava stared into her lo mein, avoiding looking twice; even though she wanted to.

"In Ohio. Working a hunt." Tito answered as he rounded the back of the room. Ava watched him pull down a target.

"So, how'd it go?" Mal came over and sat next to her with his container of sweet and sour chicken.

"I whooped his ass." Ava smiled.

Dallas rolled his eyes. "Easy there, kitten. You did good, but your training has only just begun."

Ava watched him as he grabbed a container and found a spot on the barbell bench.

"So, what is this, like...your lair?" Ava said as she fished around for a noodle.

"Well, when you say it like that, it sounds evil." Mal smirked, his brown eyes lighting up with laughter.

"What defines good and evil, Mal?" She nudged him playfully as sarcasm dripped in her tone.

"Is that what they teach you in college? To sound smart, you just have to rephrase everything as a question?" He jabbed her back.

"The answer to that is simple." Ava watched Tito throw his knife at the target.

"Do tell."

"We're the good guys because we *kill* the bad guys. They're the bad guys because they kill innocent people."

Ava watched the knife as it landed in the middle of the target.

The room fell silent.

"Heard there's going to be a memorial service for your friend, and the other victims," Mal said, breaking the silence.

"Yeah, this weekend." Ava tensed.

"You gonna go?" Mal pushed.

"Why do you care?" She bristled.

Dallas's eyes caught hers, and for a moment it looked as if he understood. Which was really weird. Dallas wasn't the sentimental type.

The sight made her wonder...

"You think those guys from Alpha Pi are going to be there? The ones from the pizza shop?" Mal was serious.

"I   don't   know...maybe?"   She shrugged.

"They're vamps, Ava." Mal looked at her, glancing down at her wrist.

"How do you know?" She cocked an eyebrow.

"Because we've been tracking the one for a few states now," Vinny spoke up.

"But..." Ava set her chopsticks down, remembering Liam and his friends coming into the lecture hall, from *outside*. At two o'clock in the afternoon, with the sun out, when Liam passed her in the quad a few weeks ago. "But they walk around during the day. I thought vampires like...incinerated in the sun." She looked down at Mal.

"Some do. Some don't. I'm not really sure *why* that is, but that's myth buster number one. Some vampires can walk in the daylight, making them much more deadly, and less likely to be detected unless you're a trained professional." Mal smiled at her.

"What else should I know? About them?" Ava hedged, her curiosity piqued.

"They're not all that hard to kill, but they are hard to trap. Pretty much anything that could kill a person, could kill a bloodsucker. The only difference is, you have to burn them immediately, or they'll heal their wounds. Fire is their worst enemy."

"So...do I like, get a stake now? Or a knife? Like the movies?"

Dallas chuckled.

"I don't know if that's a wise idea..." Mal's shoulders tensed.

"Why the hell not? At least she can protect herself with one," Dallas said through a mouthful of fried rice.

"I feel like you're going to need a bit more experience before you go throwing knives like Vinny or staking anyone in the chest. You can seriously hurt yourself if you don't know what you're doing. Especially if you're not capable of fending off their thrall." Mal glanced at Dallas. "I assume you told her about their thrall?" He raised an eyebrow.

Dallas who nodded in response. "Lesson number one—Vampire Jedi Mind Tricks. The college course you'll never find in the books." He smirked.

"What's lesson number two?" Vinny said with a chuckle.

"Lesson number two—Mal finished chewing his food. "Is how to fight the bloody Jedi's mind tricks. How to ground yourself." He looked at Ava. "You have to have a strong mind to fight them too, Ava. It isn't just about strength and adrenaline."

For a moment Ava could see the fear and worry cross Mal's face, as his lips frowned. "And you think I don't have a strong mind?" She couldn't help the disdain that laced her voice.

"Quite the opposite, actually. You're one of the most stubborn people I know, and come hell or high water, when you have your heart set on something..." He smiled, but it wasn't genuine.

"We just need to recalibrate all that power of will."

Ava looked down at her brother, and suddenly she felt like she was ten again. Asking him to help her with her homework. Asking him to teach her how to throw a punch because she wanted to deck Maddox Corsol in the face for pushing around her friend. "You'll teach me how though, right?"

Mal pursed his lips, and the expression on his face was worried. But he replaced it quickly with confidence, even if it was false.

"Of course, Simba." Mal reached out and held her wrist softly. "It's my fault you're in this mess in the first place." he whispered, and Ava tightened her grip on his wrist in return.

When he let go of her wrist, they ate the rest of their dinner in silence.

CHAPTER TWENTY-TWO

AVA SAT ON the ground, her eyes closed, legs crossed. The long blades of grass tickled her knees through the frayed holes in her jeans. It was driving her crazy.

"Focus." Mal's voice was calm.

"I can't focus if you keep nagging at me to focus," she grumbled.

"Tune me out then. You should be good at that." She could hear the laughter in his voice.

"Should I say *ommm* or something?" She could feel her lips cracking a smile of her own.

"Fuck you."

She felt Mal shove her. She opened her eyes and couldn't help but laugh. "Obviously your mind isn't as strong as you think it is if you can't *ignore* me." She shoved him back.

"I'm serious, Ava. You need to be able to block out everything. Focus on *one* thing in your mind. Something to ground you." Mal brought his knees up to his chest, wrapping his arms around them. His dark hair hung in his face and she noted how long it was.

It seemed Mal had forgone the cut and clean look in the past year and embraced the grunge look. It added to his "rockstar cover" she presumed.

He was silent for a moment, as if he was contemplating something.

"Why so serious, Mal?" She tried to joke with him once more, knowing he'd usually bite on a Batman reference.

"I never told you the truth, Ava." His voice was serious, and all joking, casual tones cast aside brought Ava to alertness.

"What do you mean?" she asked as she scooted closer to her brother, backing herself up against the retaining wall in the backyard of the estate. She sat shoulder to shoulder with him, and he turned to her, and she could see the tears starting to form.

"About mom and dad. What really happened that night?"

Oh. Oh no, Mal...

Ava swallowed nervously. It wasn't as if she couldn't talk about it. She *wished* someone could talk about it. Their aunt never mentioned them. Mal hadn't said a word about them since the funeral. It was like they wanted to pretend it didn't happen. That maybe they were on a long vacation somewhere or something.

Ava knew everyone grieved differently, but she wished just for once, *someone* would talk about how awful her mom's chicken tetrazzini was, or how her dad always lost on board game night. She thought that maybe it would help with the nightmares. Bring her some sort of closure.

"Mal—"

"It was vampires, Ava. They were killed by vamps." His voice shook as he said the words. He couldn't look at her.

The words sunk in. *Vampires.*

"In Massachusetts?" Ava said with surprise.

Mal's lips lifted only a fraction.

"Bloodsuckers are everywhere, Ava. They don't just exist here."

Ava nodded. "Oh."

"I found out...what happened. That's when I decided to become a slayer. I wanted to avenge them." Mal's eyes focused on the dandelions blowing in the breeze in the yard.

"You wanted to find the vamp who did it. That's why you were always leaving, wasn't it? You were looking for them." Ava's gaze settled on the setting sun.

"Yeah. I'm still looking." Mal reached his hand down and picked up hers. His fingers brushed her bite mark gently.

"You're lucky, Ava. I don't think you know how lucky you are." His voice was soft.

Ava pulled her wrist from his touch, running her own fingers over the shimmering scar. "He saved my life, Mal. I know that. I was attacked, by *other* vamps. I didn't know that's what they were, but it makes sense now. The one, he—" Her voice caught in her throat. "He cut me, with a knife. Was bleeding me out. They left, and I—"

Mal wrapped his arms around her and pulled her close. "You don't have to tell me if you don't want to, Ava." He ran his hands over her knotted windblown hair.

"No. I need you to understand what happened to me." She said the words out loud, but a part of her was certain it wasn't Mal who needed to understand. *She* needed to understand.

"They left, and I don't know how long they were gone. It could have been hours, minutes. Time stood still. I was dying. I know that." She leaned against her brother, his warmth a comfort. "Then the door opened. I heard voices, and I thought... I only had one thought." She could feel tears forming behind her own eyes.

"He emerged from the shadows like some angel. He wasn't alone, though. The guy he was with wanted to leave, and I saw my chance. I didn't want to waste it."

The moment was so vivid to her, as if she were there. Mal's hold on her the only thing grounding her to this world, as she relived the moment that changed her entire life.

"I asked him to save Ross. I tried to move, but my legs were like dead weight. He told me..." She remembered the glowing green eyes, the way his fingers brushed her skin.

The way her stomach flipped when he looked at her. She ran her fingers over her wrist absentmindedly and felt a strange loyalty within her blood as she remembered him. The man...no, *vampire* that saved her life.

Cassius.

He'd asked her permission first, though she hadn't truly understood what he was asking.

The word echoed in her head; *vampire.* Bloodsucking monsters.

Vampires killed her parents. Her boyfriend.

But one of them also...saved her life.

They couldn't all be ruthless killers...could they?

"He marked you. He may have saved your life at the moment, but..."

Ava looked up at Mal in question.

"But what?" She whispered.

"But it's still a death mark, Ava. One day he's going to have to make good on his claim." His eyes settled on hers and she could see the pain there.

Ava closed her eyes, and suddenly she knew exactly what she needed to ground her. "Is it our parents, that you think about? When you fight them?" she whispered.

"Yes." Mal's voice darkened.

"And that helps you defeat them?" She looked up at him once more.

Mal nodded in response.

"My blood belongs to me. I won't let anyone change that," she said with much more confidence than she felt at the moment.

Mal smiled lightly.

"I might be marked, as you say, but I'm not going down without a fight."

"Then you're going to need to master the art of slaying." He smiled, and this time it was genuine.

"Okay, Mister Miyagi. Teach me the ways of the slayer, and one day I'll help you take down the vamps that killed our parents."

"Okay, grasshopper. But first..." He pulled his arm from her shoulder and rose from his spot on the ground as he looked at his watch. "You need to finish your paper, and I need to meet up with Dallas and the boys, for a jam session."

Mal stretched as he spoke.

"I thought the amp was just a prop?" She rose from her seat as well.

"Nope. We *do* actually play instruments. Just not as often as we would like."

"Does your little band have a name?" she prodded.

Mal smirked at her. "Well, it's changed a couple times. Now we're Blood Of My Enemy."

Ava rolled her eyes. "Lame. You can do better than that."

Mal chuckled.

"The ladies don't think its lame." They walked in through the sliding glass door.

"Eew. You're disgusting, you know that." She bristled at the idea of Mal and groupies.

"Why, thank you. I'll take that as a

compliment," he said as they parted ways for the evening.

CHAPTER TWENTY-THREE

CASSIUS SLID HIS hands in his pockets as he walked through the doors of St. Stephens Church. The service was for Ross Parish, the first victim in what the news was calling, The Chester University Murders, yet there were flowers and paper signs, and mementos left outside of the church, littering its parking lot, for the twin girls who'd been taken as well. Unsurprisingly the press had shown up, newscasters and reporters milling about the place amidst the large crowd of college students, and likely Ross's family.

The church smelled of an array of flora, as the bouquets lined the central stage around a podium, with a large photograph of Ross. Tawny skin, dark brown eyes, perfectly groomed facial hair, and a coif of dark brown hair that reminded Cassius of the hairstyles he'd seen prevalent on humans in the 1950's.

When I lived with Eden.

Why was it after all these years, the memories came back to him?

He hadn't left Italy on the brightest of terms with her. He'd told no one of his plan, not even his mother. Or Leon.

The memories tried to weasel their way into his psyche. Memories of crowded rooms, fluffed skirts, and dark eyes as the music buzzed. Things were different then.

I was different then.

Cassius took his seat in the back of the room, sliding into a pew as he gazed around the room, hoping to find a familiar face. After all, he could feel her pulse alive and well.

When his eyes found her, he saw that she was not alone.

She was with the man from the pizza shop, and someone else. A tall, dark-haired man, with blue eyes, who looked like he could give Taj a run for his money in the lifting department.

And then he saw *them.*

Liam, Brody, and Logan, and what he gathered were the other members of the fraternity. They all had that same look that the fraternities often bore. They wore dress khakis, and each one of them boasted green and white shirts, covered with blazers and gold pins that bore the crest of their fraternity.

They've got a lot of nerve, showing up here.

Cassius watched as they all took their seats, and the echoes in the church started to die down.

He focused ahead as the priest started to mill about his podium, waiting for everyone to quiet, and he could feel her gaze from across the room. A part of him did not want to look at her; after all, he could feign that he did not know she'd be there, or quite possibly that he hadn't seen her if she approached him.

Surely, he'd mastered better control than this; after all, he'd stayed off fresh blood likely longer than this woman had been alive. He'd prided himself on his ability to reign in his monstrous instincts. It was safer. But yet despite knowing these things, despite knowing he should refrain from doing so, Cassius met her gaze.

She didn't look as pissed as he thought she would, and that made him feel a sense of relief. She just...stared at him. Amber eyes of fire, deep and inviting. Long, dark hair falling over her shoulder, down her back. Her eyes fixed him to his spot, for a moment longer, before turning back to her companions.

CHAPTER TWENTY-FOUR

AVA SAT THROUGH the service with her brother, and that was enough. It wasn't that she was particularly uncomfortable, after all, she'd only been dating Ross for a month. It wasn't like she was in love with him or anything. But it was the first funeral service she'd attended since her parents.

The memories pushed forth, of the night she'd found them, and she breathed deeply.

The sight of the blood on the carpet.

Her father's eyes—dead, and glassy.

Her mother's lifeless body.

Ava sucked in a breath, as the vivid memory pushed forth.

Mal's eyes were not quite fixed on the podium, with the speeches from all the students, and friends of Ross's. No. Mal scanned the crowd for vampiric threats. Dallas quietly took her hand, not saying a word. The small gesture, kind as it was, was not one she'd expect from him. She let it rest on top of hers, his warmth enveloping her, though her wrist already burned with heat where fangs had marked her. It seemed that her body knew Cassius was near before she could even consider the idea.

The notion both angered her and

brought her a strange peace. She'd have to ask Mal if that was normal, for marked individuals who had bites like hers. Ones that didn't turn or kill.

Would her wrist flare with heat like this every time he was near?

You act as if you'll see him again.

She shifted against Dallas in the pew, her long, bare legs bristling against his slacks.

When the service ended, she had every intention of finding Cassius. Giving him a piece of her mind. After all she had told him to...

To what exactly?

Leave me alone?

Take his hot, crazy delusional ass elsewhere?

Ava hated to admit, that while she was certain she couldn't trust the man...*vampire*...there was something about him that intrigued her, and she knew that was a dangerous road to travel.

Flashes of the night of the party filtered in her brain.

Ava was well aware she was being moved. She felt strong arms around her, dark whispers above her.

"You're fucking insane. Just...leave her here. They'll take care of her." The voice was faded, garbled by her own distortion.

"I'm not leaving her." The voice that spoke was close, and she could feel its warmth.

"If you're not going to help me, then you can leave." The voice was steady.

"She's lost a ton of blood."

"My venom will seal the cuts. It'll just

take some time."

The feeling of abrasive fabric on her sensitive skin hurt like a bitch. The darkness pulled her under once more.

"You okay, kitten?" Dallas's voice broke through her thoughts.

"Huh?" She blinked, filtering in the world around her once more.

"You looked a little...spaced out there for a minute." Dallas leaned against the wall, his large stature set against the vases of flowers lining the hallway making him look even bigger than he actually was.

"Yeah, I'm fine." She forced a smile.

"It's okay if you're not, you know. You can tell me. I won't tell anyone." His lips turned up in a slight smile.

"We...weren't that serious or anything." She fell against the wall next to him as they waited for Mal to come back from scouting the area.

"Maybe not, but you were there when it happened, right?" He looked over at her, and she could see his eyes bore a look of sympathy.

A strange realization overcame her.

Who did you lose, Dallas?

Ava watched the crowd disperse, students mingling about. She whispered softly, "Yes."

"You did the right thing, keeping the details to yourself," he whispered back.

"Did I, though?" She looked up at him.

"It's one of the hardest things about this life. It's not something you can just...be upfront about. Most people don't know monsters exist, and it's better that way. Think about it. As far as

Ross's parents know, their son died. They might not know the details, but would you want them to? You were there. You know them." Dallas's voice was solid as he spoke.

"No. Not really." Ava frowned, remembering the scream of pain that came after the moan of ecstasy.

"They have their closure. Enough to be able to try and move through the loss. Live life normally again someday."

Ava ran her fingers over her wrist, noting that her skin felt normal. No tingling sensation of ice or heat. Just...*normal.*

Which meant *he* was gone.

"But I know. The truth," she whispered.

"You plan on doing something about it?" Dallas raised an eyebrow at her.

"What can I do, Dallas?" She shrugged, her gaze fixated on his deep blue pools of startling sympathy.

"You can get justice, Ava." His voice was solid and unwavering, and carried a hint of darkness that spoke to Ava's very soul.

"How?" she asked seriously.

"You can take out the vamp that murdered your boyfriend."

He's serious.

"I barely know what I'm doing. Okay, yeah, I was able to knock you around *a little*, maybe I'll figure out this grounding thing too, but—"

"Mal's your brother. It's his natural instinct to protect you. He'll teach you defense, sure. But you need more than defense." Dallas slid his hands into his pockets nonchalantly.

"And let me guess, you're just to person to teach me, aren't you, Dallas?" She licked her lips and a smile started to form.

"I am quite a formidable opponent, kitten. No one slays quite like I do." His eyes twinkled.

"Really laying it on thick there aren't you?" She let out a chuckle.

"Is it working?" His eyes lit up only a little.

Ava rolled her eyes. "As long as I get a stake, or a knife. I'm in."

"Kitten, by the time I'm done with you, you'll be able to kill a vamp with your bare hands."

"Is there a crash course option? I'd like to be able to kill this bloodsucker before he strikes again." She leaned closer to Dallas, their hushed voices emitting heat in the closed space.

"I'll pick you up tonight, say...nine?"

"You're not going to be with Mal?" Ava's eyes settled on his lips, and her heart started to race.

"I'm a big boy, Ava. I don't need Mal to chaperone me everywhere I go." The sparkle in his eye was mischievous but also alluring.

"It's a date." She smiled sweetly,

"They're gone." Mal's voice broke the silence and Ava moved away from Dallas once more and settled her gaze on her brother.

"Damn assholes are harder to trap than I thought they would be." Mal ran a hand through his hair, his frustration evident.

"Mal! You're in a church!" Ava poked him.

"Seriously, Ava?" Mal regarded her with an annoyed glare.

"Have some respect, Mal." Dallas smirked as he ribbed him.

"Fuck the both of you," Mal grumbled as he sauntered off toward the exit, leaving Ava and Dallas laughing in his dust.

CHAPTER TWENTY-FIVE

"YOUR IDEA OF a training session is Russo's Sports Bar?" Ava raised an eye at Dallas as she dismounted from the back of his bike.

Dallas ran his hand through his short brown hair, after setting his helmet on the handlebar, and kicking down the kickstand on the glistening curb on Chester's main street.

"Well, for starters, I need to gauge

your aim, and Russo's has what we need. Darts, axe throwing—"

"You could have just taken me to your top-secret Bat Cave." Ava shrugged as she sauntered toward the door.

Dallas was at her side rather quickly and opened the door for her. "Yes, I could have, but I thought just maybe you'd want some better food than take out Chinese." He smirked at her.

Ava rolled her eyes. "If I didn't know any better, I'd think you were trying to hit on me, Dallas," she joked with him as they walked into the restaurant.

"Kitten, if I wanted to hit on you, trust me, you'd know. There'd be no question." He smiled mischievously as he brushed past her to a high top table.

Ava shook her head and followed.

Russo's wasn't the only sports bar in

Chester, but it was the only sports bar that boasted billiards, a dart wall, axe throwing, and an extensive beer menu.

Ave leaned languidly against the high top as she picked up the menu.

The waitress came over rather quickly. "What can I get you...two?" she asked sweetly.

Ava didn't miss the look of judgement on her face.

"I'll take whatever beer you have on special." Dallas smiled, showcasing his perfect teeth, and his eyes lit up brightly.

The waitress seemed to ease up a bit. "That all, darlin'?" she drawled.

Ava rolled her eyes.

"A bucket of buffalo wings, with a side of ranch?" He raised an eyebrow at Ava, who shrugged.

"And what will you have to drink,

sweetie?" The waitress did her best to sound nice, but Ava could tell she was judging her.

"I'll have a water, thanks," Ava grumbled. When the waitress finally left, she slammed down her menu. "Can I ask you an honest question, Dallas?" Ava spoke up.

"Kitten, you can ask me anything, you know that." Dallas pulled out a few darts from the abandoned dartboards. The place wouldn't even start coming alive until ten.

"How long have you been...you know. Doing the vamp thing?" She leaned against the tabletop, watching Dallas collect the darts. She didn't miss the opportunity to let her gaze drift upon his ass. In his dark wash jeans, she couldn't help but appreciate it. It's not like he could see her looking, anyway.

"Since I was about your age." He walked over to her with a handful of yellow and red darts.

"You ever train anyone?" She shifted her weight as he organized the darts by color.

"Yellow or Red?" He glanced up at her.

The waitress dropped off their drinks hurriedly.

"Red." Ava took a sip of her water.

"I *trained* Vinny." He shrugged.

"Vinny's the one who looks like a lost member of The Cure, right?" Ava smirked.

Dallas let out a chuckle as he picked up a dart, and took his stance, his vision fixating on the dartboard.

"I'm surprised you even know who

The Cure are." He threw his dart, and it landed with a bulls eye.

"I know a lot of things, *Dallas*." Her voice dripped with sarcasm.

"Right. Of course, you do, you're a *college girl*." He said the words with the utmost humor, but there was also an edge to his voice that was most...flirtatious?

"Fuck you." She twisted her lips into an amused grin.

"Quite stalling. It's your turn."

Ava picked up a dart, feeling the weight of it in her hands. She turned it around, inspecting it, before settling it in her fingers properly. She focused on the dartboard, and her wrist flared with heat. The feeling was startling, and whereas it should have been distracting to her, it only fueled her focus more.

She fixated her gaze on the dartboard as her blood boiled beneath the surface. Memories pushed forth of tongues on flesh, of blood rushing to the surface. Of razor-sharp fangs piercing her skin, and they meshed with the sight of her father's lifeless eyes, of Ross's lifeless, blood drained body that seemed to have disappeared into the ether.

She didn't think twice about throwing her dart. She didn't even realize it had left her hand, until she heard Dallas whistle.

"Not a bad shot. I can definitely work with that." He chuckled.

Ava looked to where her dart had landed. It wasn't a bulls eye like Dallas had thrown, but it was much closer than she thought she'd land.

The waitress dropped off the bucket

of wings, and sides of ranch as Dallas took a swig of his beer before picking up another dart.

"Do you like it? College, I mean," he said as he threw the dart, before diving into a wing.

"I guess, it's okay. It's an experience, you know." She shrugged as she picked up a dart.

"What's your major?" Dallas popped another wing into his mouth.

"Major in Business Administration, Minor in History." She threw her dart.

"You don't really strike me as the office type."

"Well, you don't really strike me as the musician type," she cracked.

"Your words wound me, Ava. Truly." He chuckled as he took another drink, threw another dart. "I was offered scholarships you know. For Chester, Youngstown."

Ava grabbed a wing herself and had to admit the taste was rather divine. Spicy, tangy, with just the right amount of kick, and accented by the cool taste of ranch. "Why didn't you take it? The scholarship?" She licked her fingers clean before wiping them on a napkin and grabbing another dart, but Dallas's words stopped her from throwing it.

"Because I learned the truth, the hard way. Like you." His voice had lost its air of humor and teasing.

"I'm sorry..." Ava spoke softly.

"Sometimes the world has a crazy way of showing you who you really are." Dallas picked up his glass and took a long pull of his beer.

Ava threw her dart, but this time it

didn't land as well as the others.

"Don't be sorry. I know this life isn't ideal, for anyone. But it's who I am. It's what I was meant to do. The rest of it..." Dallas threw his last dart, and it landed smack in the center, a bulls eye once more. His words hung in the air, as his gaze settled on the dartboard, his eyelashes standing out against the lights that illuminated him.

Ava sipped her water as she took in the sight of Dallas. Amidst the red and orange neon lights, she could almost see it.

A young, vibrant Dallas who had the world at his feet.

An attractive, charismatic boy next door who could have anything he wanted with that smile.

A life he never got to live, because

somehow, he'd learned monsters were real. He'd left a safe and happy life, normalcy and traded it in for flannel shirts, a microphone, and a stake.

Or maybe he's more of a knife guy like Vinny.

"Your turn, kitten." His bright blue eyes flashed at her.

Ava stilled her breath as she focused on the dartboard. She thought of the ways her life had changed, since that night at the party. Since Ross had been killed. Since Cassius had saved her life. In a way she'd been given a second chance too, much like Dallas. A chance to see into the darkness that most people didn't get to see.

She knew without a doubt, that like Dallas she'd never be able to look away.

The world around her, around *them,*

even now left her with the question of who among them was a monster? Her wrist still flared with heat, her skin prickled like goosebumps; but there was no sign of Cassius, or Liam.

She knew within her heart, she'd never be able to look at the world, at people, the same now that she knew what kind of evil lurked in the shadows. In the daylight, even.

Ava focused on her breath, on the heated blood in her veins.

On the feeling of fangs against her soft skin.

On the memories that swam in her head of bloodied bodies, and the feeling of helplessness.

She closed her eyes, and she threw the dart.

When she opened her eyes, she was

surprised, and by the tone in Dallas's voice he was surprised too, but there was also another emotion in his voice. *Pride.*

Ava's dart sat snug in the center, knocking Dallas's out of its coveted bulls eye spot.

CHAPTER TWENTY-SIX

CASSIUS RAN HIS hand through his golden hair as he paced back and forth on the patio. He'd heard Liam and his cohorts, even though he hadn't been intent on listening. A part of him was surprised to see them attend the funeral of the man they killed. Although, it was a very Boracelli thing to do, if he had to be honest.

It seemed no matter if one was a born

Boracelli or not, the disturbing trait of reveling in your kill seemed to be quite prevalent among the high covens.

That is what happens when you've truly lost your sense of humanity, I suppose.

With Halloween only two weeks away, and a crackdown at the University on Greek events, the rogue Liam and his friends were forced to draw their prey outside of their normal hunting grounds.

The fact that there had been no recent death reports was startling to Cassius. He knew better than anyone how maddening it was to starve yourself for weeks.

In the beginning, in his early days as a vampire, he'd done everything he could to resist the need to feed on human blood.

It wasn't a pleasant experience, and most certainly always ended up putting him in the guiltiest predicament.

As if his body remembered just as much as his mind, his stomach flipped with nausea.

"It's the perfect location, far enough away from the University that no one will think twice about connecting the dots but close enough for all interested parties to get to," Liam had said.

"There's a sense of drama to it, too," Logan said.

"A Halloween Party in an abandoned church on the outskirts of town? Sounds positively perfect to me." Liam smiled.

"And no one will notice a little blood, either. The girls will practically be begging for it. All keyed up on that vampire romance shit," Brody chimed in.

They'd disappeared after that.

Cassius sat in the chaise, his head in his hands. In his heart he knew he should do *something*.

At the very least, I should tell Ava. Make certain she stays clear of that party, he thought as he watched the ripple of the water in the pool.

Taj opened the sliding glass door.

"Where's Jasmine?" Cassius perked his head up.

"Some concert or something over in Willowcrest." Taj took a seat on the rubber chaise, the one that always squeaked from years worth of rust buildup.

"Surprised you didn't go with her, given your protective streak." Cassius twisted his lips.

"I'm trying not to be a dick. Cut me

some slack here, Cas." Taj kicked his legs up as he leaned back on the lounge chair. "I'm sorry I went off on you the other day." Taj's voice was low, but genuine. The man was never very good at admitting his faults.

He was a damn loyal, good friend, though. Even if he didn't have a filter.

"Apology accepted." Cas smirked.

"It's just—"

Cassius's smile faltered.

"We've been friends, what thirty some years? I know you better than I knew my own brothers and sisters. I know you have this hero fixation and all, but damn it, Cassius, you can't save them all. Some things are just beyond your control." Taj breathed deeply.

"I know that, Taj. But I can't just sit here in isolation either. I must live my life too. I can't stay scared for the rest of eternity that Eden will find me." His voice hung on her name.

Cassius wished life had been different. He wished so many times that Eden would see the light, but she never did. But he knew the darkness had poisoned her heart long ago.

When she'd lost the only man she ever truly loved, along with a life she never knew she wanted.

Marcellus Medici.

They'd grieved their losses together, gotten close even. Close enough that he'd let her in. That he'd shelved his fear of his Aurelian curse and made love to her anyway.

And then I'd found out the truth.

Cassius ran his hand through his hair. The memory of their last moments, the moment he knew she'd never truly love him, but she wouldn't let anyone else have him either, forced its way through his brain.

"I am not some pawn in your games of dominance, Eden. I am more than some fucking stud for you to parade and commandeer." He turned toward the door, giving his back to her.

"So help the gods, Cassius Aurelia, if you walk out that door..." Her voice was cold, devoid of any emotion she'd once held for him. She no longer cared for anyone, really. She'd lost too much, suffered too much, and the pain, the bloodlust had driven her insane. *"I will not give you the choice next time. You will obey me."* She growled at him.

He turned to her, taking in the sight of her violet-rimmed eyes that glowed against her pale skin. She stood there in the tower, amidst the stone and tapestries, dressed in the most exquisite plum silk dress, her long, thin legs milky white against the darkness and shadows. With her dark raven hair running over her shoulders like a waterfall, Cassius had to admit that her beauty was only surface value.

Nothing beautiful was left inside of Eden Boracelli's heart.

He'd deluded himself into thinking there was for too long.

She didn't value life anymore. Not his, or anyone else's but her own. She only valued what she could control. Her desire to be Queen was nothing more than a desire to control everything, and everyone around her. Including him.

He'd almost given her an heir, on more

than one occasion.

But she did not love *him. There was nothing anymore that she could give him, that he wanted, and even if there was...*

She had blood on her hands.

His father's blood, to be exact.

It would have been so easy to hurt her, so very easy to bring her castle crumbling to the ground. But that was a choice he had made. If he had given in to the need to hurt, the need to make her understand the depth of his disdain for her...he would be no better than her.

"There is always a choice. The fact you fail to understand that is why I will never be yours. You cannot control me, Eden."

"You've got to let it go, Cas. You can't fix everything. You're only one person. Marking Ava..." Taj took a deep breath.

"You made yourself *and her* a ticking timebomb. The Boracelli's will certainly be waiting for you to make your move. You *should* just...enjoy her. Savor the blood, and anything else you might want from her." Taj let out a dark laugh, and Cassius's back straightened.

"I don't want any such things from her, I assure you." His voice was short.

"Right. And I'm the queen of fucking England." Taj let out a laugh.

Cassius sighed.

"It's okay you know. You're allowed to *want* her blood. I mean, you did put a claim on it. You're allowed to *want* to fuck her too. It's *normal* to feel and want those things. It's what we're made for. It doesn't make you the bad guy." The way Taj said the words were solid, and Cassius knew they were true.

It was normal. Sex and blood were two sides of the same coin for monsters like himself. He could feel her in his blood, in his veins. A steady pulse of life.

That was all he wanted for her.

For himself, even.

To live.

Liam and his cohorts were planning a Halloween smorgasbord of blood, sex, and death, and in that moment, Cassius knew there was only one thing he truly wanted.

He'd tell Ava about the party.

He'd try to save as many as he could.

Even if it meant going against his own kind.

CHAPTER TWENTY-SEVEN

THE MAN IN the shadows stared at her. His eyes followed her no matter where she moved.

"You let me die," the shadow spoke.

"I was dying too!" she yelled at the darkness.

The shadows moved, forming into a shape, and then a body.

Ross.

"You look pretty alive to me." His voice

was thick with anger.

"I'm sorry..." Her legs felt like dead weight. She couldn't move them.

Ross stalked closer to her, his blue and white checkered shirt stained with blood.

Why did the shirt look so familiar?

She remembered exactly what he wore. A red shirt and khakis.

"You didn't even try..." He stood above her, and his eyes flickered from brown to green, then brown again.

"I did try!" she hollered back.

"Lies!" His eyes glowed green, and sharp, white fangs glistened as he opened his mouth.

"You knew what happened to me, and you did nothing..."

"There was nothing I could do!" Ava could feel the tears forming in her eyes.

"He's still out there..." Ross looked in the distance, and Ava could see the shining beacon of light coming from the top of the stairs.

"Who?" Her voice cracked.

"The monster who killed me," he answered.

He turned back to her, but this time he had shifted into someone else.

Something else.

Cassius stood before her, his green eyes soft and bright even in the darkness.

Ross's words echoed in the air. The monster who killed me.

Her wrist burned with heat, and her breathing hitched.

Serenity befell her, and all she wanted was to submit to it. Feel its peace.

But the cries of death rang in the air.

Ross's broken voice.

There would be no peace.

Not tonight.

Ava awoke in her bed and felt the coldness of the air kiss her skin. She looked at her alarm clock, and could see the red digital letters read three am. She let out a breath as she stared at the ceiling. It had been quite a while since she'd had a nightmare such as this. She took a breath once more.

One. Two. Three...

The images still swirled around in her head. Of an angry, bloodied Ross. Of the beautiful monster who'd saved her life.

Dallas was right. She'd never be able to look at things the way they'd been before Ross was killed.

Before she'd learned the truth that monsters were real.

Perhaps it was guilt, or...perhaps it was just that she was drawn to the shadows, and what lay beyond them. She was a Crowley, after all. Darkness, and the affinity for supernatural things was in her blood.

Whatever it was, Ava knew for certain she wouldn't be able to rest until justice had been served. There would be no peace for Ross's soul, or hers, until she knew his killer had been served. And so, Ava closed her eyes, and focused on the sound of her breath, on the steady beat of her heart, until she found sleep once more.

***

The aroma of coffee in the air was divine to Ava's senses and was almost enough to make her forget her terrible nightmare.

"I don't know how you can drink that sludge," Mal grumbled as he threw his flannel shirt on over top of a plain black shirt.

Ava sipped her coffee slowly as she noticed the stubble making a comeback on his face. Despite his recent shower, he still looked scruffy and unkempt. "I don't know how anyone functions without it," she chided as she followed him out the door, travel mug in hand.

"It's called stamina, Ava." Mal opened the driver side door of his car and wasted no time.

Ava fell into the passenger seat with a scowl. "You are the last person who should be giving a lecture on stamina, Mal. You can barely hang around here for longer than—"

"Dallas tells me you have good aim," he said as he started the car, and pulled out quickly.

"Did he now?" Ava pursed her lips. It shouldn't have bothered her, that Dallas told Mal about their little date.

It wasn't a date.

It absolutely wasn't a date because that would make me the worst person in the world. Going out on a date right after your dead boyfriend's service with another man who's over a decade older than you.

No, it certainly wasn't a date. It was just a meeting of the minds to discuss her inevitable training. Dallas had mentioned he'd trained Vinny to hunt the evil bloodsuckers, and Ava knew without a doubt the chord had been struck within her as well.

"He did. Suggested we test out your ability with actual weapons, see what sticks." Mal stared through the windshield, and Ava got the feeling he was hiding something.

Mal fiddled with the knobs on his radio, and Ava decided not to press him. Not yet anyway. If he was truly hiding something, she'd get to the bottom of it.

When Mal pulled up to the Bat Cave, Ava noticed three motorcycles parked out front.

"I was under the impression it was just going to be a brother sister bonding day." She sighed.

"What's the matter, Ava? Scared you won't be able to hang with the big boys?" Mal shut the door, and a light chuckle escaped his throat.

"Oh, I can hang, Mal. I'm just worried

your friends will laugh at you when I beat your ass." She smiled as she made a beeline for the door.

"Keep that enthusiasm. You're going to need it when you come face to face with those bloodsucking leeches." Mal's tone took on a darker tone as he opened the door for her.

"After you," he said as he motioned for her to enter.

As Ava entered the gym, she could see the ring was occupied with two shirtless, sweaty men who happened to be rolling around legs locked onto one another.

"Go ahead, fucking tap..." the one on top growled, blonde hair falling in his face.

Tito, Ava reminded herself of his name. The one who was throwing knives before.

"Never!" the man underneath roared back as he threw Tito back with force, knocking him to the ground. Vinny stood up, cracking his neck, his steely grey eyes glancing at her as he smiled. Tito took advantage of the distraction and kicked his leg out from under him.

Ava couldn't help but let out a laugh.

Mal opened a cabinet in the corner, and Ava could see quite the collection of blades, stakes and weapons that looked primarily medieval.

The sight alone excited her, but she was soon pulled from her anticipation as a sweat soaked, shirtless Dallas came traipsing around the corner.

Ava couldn't help as her eyes roved over his defined chest, noting the twin star tattoos on each side above his pecs;

his hips cutting the most delicious angle, that perfect v shape that was usually only afforded to male models and athletes. Ava felt her mouth run dry at the sight, and so she forced herself to look away.

Hell Ava, get a hold of yourself.

She grabbed the knife out of Mal's hand.

"Hey—"

"Enough deliberating, Mal. Let's do this," she said as she took a stance she hoped was formidable enough.

CHAPTER TWENTY-EIGHT

AVA PATTED HER hair dry with the towel, her bare feet padding along the cool hardwood floor in the hallway, when the sound of a doorbell alerted her.

It seemed Becky had vacated the premises for the evening, in favor of a wine night with her friends—a weekly event in which they gossiped about their children's love lives.

Though Becky didn't have any

children, that didn't deter her from incessantly trying to match Ava with any of her friends' sons, or their friends' sons, and so forth.

You just need to meet a nice boy, and settle down, she had said on numerous occasions. Connie was just as bad.

It was one of the reasons Ava was glad to leave—and why she was so nervous about the idea of bringing Ross home for the holidays if everything went as planned.

But things didn't go as planned, and that was her cross to bear.

She threw the towel in the hamper in the hallway before quickening her pace to the door.

When she opened it, her eyes widened in surprise.

"What the fuck are *you* doing here? I

thought I told you—"

"May I come in?" Cassius's lips turned up in a slight smile.

Ava twisted her lips and raised an eyebrow at him.

"If I said no, would that prevent you from coming inside?" She crossed her arms.

Cassius's green eyes sparkled.

"Of course not, but it would be rather rude if I just *walked* in without being invited, now, wouldn't it?"

Ava considered his words and decided instead to meet him on the porch.

She ran a hand through her wet hair, pushing it behind her.

Cassius's eyes dilated only a fraction before returning to normal.

Well, that's kind of strange.

"What are you doing on my front

porch?" She didn't mince her words.

"I needed to see you." He cleared his throat.

Ava gazed at him skeptically.

"Does that work on all your victims?" she bit.

Cassius looked offended.

"I can assure you, Ava, I do not go around stalking young women as you may think." He crossed his arms, and the motion brought her attention to his long, slender arms, the slight curve of his bicep. Her wrist flared with heat, her skin with goosebumps, and her heart beat faster.

Fight it, Ava.

She blinked furiously, before meeting his gaze, and remembered the sound of Ross's pained scream.

"Could have fooled me," she drawled.

"The vampires that...harmed you..."

Ava's attention was on high alert at his words.

"You know who they are?" She stood a little straighter, and noticed she came up to Cassius's chest.

Somehow, she'd made it closer to him, and the realization made her take a step back. She fought to look away, but she did not win the fight.

Glowing green eyes gazed upon her, and she could not deny the sight, the way he looked at her—caused her stomach to tie in knots, and her legs to tighten.

It's just his natural defense.

But isn't thrall supposed to make my brain...foggy?

She didn't feel particularly confused.

But she did feel *something.*

A racing heart, an increased pulse.

Wetness blossomed between her legs.

Fucking hell, I need to be stronger than this.

"I do. And I know that they are planning to strike again." Cassius licked his lips, and the sight was like a shockwave directly to her groin.

Ava shifted her weight. "Why should I believe anything you say?" Her eyes flickered to his lips, remembering their soft feel on her skin, his fangs puncturing her wrist.

The memory of it was not...*unpleasant.*

"Because I—"

Cassius could not finish his sentence, for he was punched square in the jaw by a rather pissed off Mal.

CHAPTER TWENTY-NINE

IT HAD BEEN quite a long time since anyone *punched* Cassius in the face. He'd been in his fair share of brawls, what with his frequent stints in and out of bars, taverns, and even hotels throughout his life, but it was usually because he was *breaking up* a fight, not instigating one.

He rubbed his jaw, and the dark-haired man drew his blade.

The very blade he'd seen in the back of the red Chevelle outside the pizza place on campus.

"Mal don't!" Ava put her hands up, and the man looked at her with question.

"Ava he's—"

"I know, Mal. He's...the one. The one who—"

"Bit you?" Mal growled and rushed toward Cassius once more.

"*Saved* me." Ava stood between Cassius and the man she called Mal.

Cassius couldn't help but notice the expanse of her figure, how her curves cut a most luscious silhouette against the fading sun. How his body responded to the sight, how he could feel her pulse quickening within him. His cock twitched, and he swallowed harshly, his mouth suddenly dry with thirst.

No, you can't. You have to fight the thoughts.

Mal's eyes widened, and he pursed his lips, looking from Ava to Cassius.

"Put the blade away," Ava spoke slowly.

Mal gazed at him with anger, fury.

"If you even so much as *try* to touch her—"

Ava scowled at Mal.

"Fuck off, Mal. I don't need you to protect me," she snapped.

I will protect you, my sweet Avarice.

"As I was saying," Cassius spoke up, drawing both of their attention.

"The vampires who hurt you—" Cassius's gaze fell over Ava for a moment, before glancing back at Mal. "— they plan to strike again. At a party off campus. In an abandoned church off route sixty." He stood straight, his voice conveying no anger or offense, despite the fact he'd just been assaulted by a pissed off human.

He has every right to be pissed, you bit someone he cares about.

It was then that the puzzle pieces came together for Cassius. Mal *knew* what he was.

The blade from the Chevelle's backseat.

A hunter's blade.

The similarities in Mal and Ava's features.

Mal was a hunter...and Ava's sibling.

Cassius let out a small breath.

Of course, this would be just my luck. Danger should have been my middle name.

"That's by the—"

"Bat Cave," Ava whispered.

"Bat Cave?" Cassius cocked his head to the side.

"When?" Mal ignored his question.

"Hallows' Eve," Cassius answered to Mal, never taking his eyes off Ava.

"I'll be there," Ava said, breaking his gaze.

This is not how I imagined this going...

"That is a terrible idea." Cassius felt his own blood starting to heat, a feeling he hadn't felt in quite some time.

Since Eden...

"Well, I wasn't really asking your opinion, Cas." Ava shot him a glare which should have been angry, or pissy, but it wasn't either of those things.

In fact, Cassius thought it was rather...alluring.

It's just the mark talking, nothing more, he tried to convince himself.

"You're not ready yet," Mal shot her a worried glance.

"I don't need your permission, either, Mal. I'm an adult."

"You're fucking eighteen, Ava. You're a child!" Mal grumbled.

Cassius felt a shock in his blood.

Eighteen?

The realization made him flush, but due to the lack of human blood in his veins, he was certain no one could distinguish any color to his cheeks.

Corpse blood didn't light up his blush quite the same way human blood did.

"I'm going to that party, and I'm going to put a fucking stake through the vamp that killed my boyfriend, and then I'm going to—" Ava stopped abruptly.

"You're going to what?" Mal's shoulders tensed and he scowled.

"I don't have to tell you shit." She turned around and faced Cassius.

"This makes us even." She gazed up at him and in her amber eyes, he could see the flecks of gold. In the dying sunlight, with heat in her eyes, Cassius's entire being felt...*alive.*

She was so close. Close enough he could reach out, touch her. Run his hands through her wet, dark hair. Trace his fingertips down her soft skin, feeling her warmth.

Close enough to kiss.

To bite.

He forced himself to look away at the thought.

"I do not think it is a wise idea for you to put yourself in danger," he whispered to her.

"Maybe I like a little danger," she whispered back.

CHAPTER THIRTY

EVERY TIME SHE closed her eyes, she saw bright, glowing green emeralds in her vision. His wet, pink tongue sliding over his perfect pout, and the memory of how it felt against the skin of her wrist pushed forth.

Ava tossed in her bed, trying to think of anything else.

When images of a sweat slicked chest, equipped with dual star tattoos washed away the memory of fangs and bliss, Ava groaned in frustration.

She looked at the alarm clock, which read three am. The witching hour.

This is fucking ridiculous. She stared at the ceiling in the darkness of her room.

Her wrist did not flare with heat, nor did her skin prickle with goosebumps.

Yet her skin was flushed and warm beneath the covers, and the thoughts of Cassius's fangs sinking into her skin, of his tongue on her flesh, made her blood *boil.*

She was safe in her bedroom, beneath her burgundy sheets. Safe, and alone. There was nothing and no one to fight here; except her own thoughts.

The desires that kept her awake.

It was too much to bear, and Ava

knew without a doubt she needed release.

To work out the frustrations of the evening, her anger.

To sate the spark of desire that had been ignited within her.

But she knew better. Vampires *killed* people.

They could not be trusted. They were the bad guys.

But yet somehow, in a way Ava could not explain, she knew Cassius was different. She couldn't stop thinking about him. She screamed a muffled sound into her pillow.

He had come to warn her. If he wanted her dead, he would not go to all the trouble of telling her such things. But what reason did he have then, to tell her not to go to the party.

Probably so he can save you for another night, when he decides he's ready to make good on his mark.

Ava had no reason to trust Cassius. But if there was even the sliver of a chance that he was telling the truth, that the vampires who hurt her, who killed Ross—if they were going to strike again, she couldn't waste the chance.

The thought of driving a stake through their chest made her heart skip a beat.

Hallows' Eve was only a week away. She knew she needed to up her training regimen, and as the thought broke through her psyche, her phone lit up with a text.

Who's texting me at three in the morning?

Your brother tells me there's going to

be a vamp attack on Hallows' Eve at the church by the gym.

Ava stared at Dallas's text and wondered if she should respond. Nothing good ever came from texts sent at three in the morning. She could feel her cheeks redden slightly, as the thought of him in the gym earlier resurfaced.

Sweat dripping down his hard abs, down the angled muscles of his hips, which cut into his shorts.

Her insides tightened.

I swear the two of you are worse than a bunch of schoolgirls.

You'd know, wouldn't you ;-)

Ava smirked, the light of her phone a beacon in the dark room.

I may have been a cheerleader, but I'm not a gossiping whore.

Dallas's text bubble faded in and out,

as if he was contemplating a response.

With that mouth of yours, I'm not quite sure I believe you.

Believe what you want. I don't kiss and tell ;-) Ava smiled.

You're going to need back up at the party.

You're not going to give me a lecture about not going?

That depends. Do you want me to lecture you?

Fuck no.

What do you want, Ava?

The question caught her off guard, and she was surprised that the answer was not a simple one.

She wanted justice—for Ross, for the other victims who had met their bitter end at the hands of monsters. She wanted to make her almost death, their deaths, count for something.

But she also could not deny she wanted to feel the blissful peace she felt with Cassius's fangs in her skin, to feel the surge of power she felt in the ring, sparring with Dallas.

But she couldn't tell him any of that.

Such deep questions you have at three in the morning. Ava hoped he would not press her.

What time do you get out of class tomorrow?

Two.

I'll pick you up. If you're going to slay your first vamp in a week, we need to make sure there's no room for error.

Oh, so another chance to beat your ass into the ring, then? Can't wait. Her lips turned up into a delicious smile.

Bring me your best, kitten. ;-)

***

Ava swung her arm out, and Dallas dodged her once again. After a solid three days of this, she had to admit her entire body was feeling the strain. Mal, Tito, and Vinny had gone out to assist Hunter, according to Dallas. It was just the two of them again.

Her tank top clung to her body like a second skin, and she could feel the strain in her muscles, in her legs, and all she wanted to do was collapse into a pile in the corner. But there would be no rest. There couldn't be.

"Come on, Ava..." Dallas taunted her as he lunged for her. She angled herself out of his way, and her long ponytail, wet from sweat, whipped around and lashed him in the face.

His hands twisted in the bottom, and he yanked her back by her hair. She fell into his embrace, the heat from his body engulfing her as he locked his arm around her, his free hand sliding over her wrist, brushing Cassius's bite mark with a familiar sting. His lips were at her ear, and she could feel the heat of his breath on her neck. She closed her eyes for only a moment, feeling the ache of her muscles as he tightened his grip, trying to focus.

"I know you're better than this," he whispered.

Ava breathed heavily, her chest rising and falling with rapid rhythm.

"Dallas..." Her voice came out much darker than she anticipated.

"You can't let them get this close..." His lips grazed her ear.

Ava's mind swam with a hundred thoughts, feelings.

She focused on only one, though. The feeling of powerlessness. The vampire who'd bled her with his knife and left her to bleed out on the concrete floor.

The sound of Ross's scream.

Ava backed herself against Dallas, the motion bringing her hands smack against his hard abs, which were slick with cold sweat. She twisted with all her might, snapping out of his hold, and she reached down into her pant leg quickly, pulling out the stake she had hidden. She lunged forth to Dallas, stake in hand as she pushed with her opposite hand and forced him back against the ring.

Her eyes burned into his gaze, and she pressed herself against him, holding him with what force she possessed against the ring.

She noted the sizeable bulge in his pants, but refused to acknowledge it at the moment, despite the fact she couldn't deny it gave her a sense of satisfaction.

"You were saying..."

Dallas let out a dark laugh.

"What's so funny?" She tried to catch her breath, but she didn't move, and he didn't relent either.

"I think you're enjoying this a little too much." He smiled darkly.

"I'm not the one who's all hot and bothered." She cast him a heated gaze.

Dallas settled his hand around hers, which held the stake against his chest, and he pulled it away slowly.

"Could have fooled me." The low

ceiling lights cast shadows on him and his defined muscles, making the sweat on his skin glisten; and all his tattoos stand out.

Her insides twisted.

And suddenly it dawned on Ava, that perhaps getting close to the vampires would be the best way to slaughter them.

It was their nature to use their thrall, to placate humans into becoming wanton little things that would allow them to get close enough to bite, to kill them. But perhaps if one thought they had her, if they could get close enough to bite her...

She'd be close enough to kill them without them realizing their mistake.

But as she looked into Dallas's bright blue eyes, she realized there were some things she just *couldn't* fight.

Because she didn't *want* to.

It all happened so fast, she couldn't be sure who made the first move.

As the stake fell from her hands, it clattered on the boxing ring floor.

Dallas's lips crushed hers with fury, his hands sliding up her back into her sweat soaked hair.

Her breasts pressed against his warm, solid chest, her hands finding their way up his arms, his neck, as her fingers traced his jaw, pulling him closer.

She slid her tongue into his mouth, and he pushed back against her, his lips traveling from her mouth to her jaw, and her heart thundered in her chest, her nerves at full attention from the adrenaline, the fight. Ava closed her eyes, and the memory of glowing green emeralds, of razor-sharp fangs biting her, pushed forth, and she couldn't help the moan that escaped her lips.

She couldn't deny that it felt good.

The fight.

The feel of Dallas's body against hers.

The building cyclone in the pit of her stomach, in her groin.

"Ava..." His voice vibrated on her skin and made her entire body flush with heat as he pulled away, catching his breath.

"Dallas..." she answered skeptically.

"Fuck..." His breath caught in his throat.

"We shouldn't do this..." He swallowed, and she could hear the concern in his voice.

"Why?" Her eyes focused on his lips,

and all she could think about was how good they felt. How badly she needed this. The release. Someone to take away all the thoughts, feelings.

Someone to make her forget.

"Why? There are a lot of reasons..." He leaned his forehead against hers, his hair tickling her face.

"What's the matter Dallas? Afraid I'll bite?" She let out a little laugh.

"Mal—"

"Doesn't need to know," she whispered, her lips brushing his again.

Dallas slid his tongue into her mouth, groaning into her before pulling away once more.

"You're—"

"A consenting adult." She kissed him again.

"Fuck...Ava..."

"If you don't want this Dallas, the door is over there..." Her heart raced; her blood boiled.

It seemed like forever until he spoke.

"I'm not going anywhere, kitten."

"Good. Neither am I."

This time when Dallas kissed her, there was no question or concern. He kissed her with fervor, with desire, and with possession.

And for the moment, Ava forgot about everything else.

About death, and monsters, and revenge.

In the arms of Jake Dallas, it was so easy to forget.

CHAPTER THIRTY-ONE

"You're sure they didn't see you?" Taj took a sip of his beer as he relaxed on the couch.

Cassius stirred the dough absentmindedly as the oven dinged. "I am certain," Cassius stopped his stirring, and he expertly spooned out drops of cookies onto the parchment lined baking sheet.

Jasmine padded down the hall, her

hair slightly disheveled from a long sleep. Cassius glanced at the clock. It was still early in the evening, only eight o'clock.

"Oh, you're baking again..." Jasmine's eyes filled with hunger.

Cassius didn't consider himself an expert baker by any means, but after spending so many years in Paris, he'd picked up the skill as a hobby and seemed to have a hard time letting it go. It helped to calm his nerves, whenever he'd feel stressed, anxious. Worried.

And he was most certainly worried about Ava attending a party in which idiotic vampires may try to challenge his claim on her or tie up *loose ends* as Brody had called her.

Taj looked at Cassius, his expression plain and simple. *Don't say anything to*

Jasmine.

Cas glanced at Jasmine's cerulean eyes and sighed. "Ava wishes to attend a party in which I know there will be vampires." He scooped out a spoonful of cookie dough, and Jasmine settled on the bar stool at the island.

Taj watched their interaction closely.

Jasmine was as exotic as the flower she was named after, and Taj treated her as such.

He'd only known her for about a decade, after she'd stumbled into the woods of Chester, an escapee of hunters.

Hunters like Mal. Ava's brother.

He hadn't mentioned his little discussion with Ava and her hunter brother to either of them, but somewhere in his depths he knew he needed to tell them. If only for the reason that by association, they would likely be made targets.

But despite knowing the danger it may put him, and even his friends in, he could not deny the truth. He would embrace whatever danger lurked beyond the woman who bore his claim on her blood.

Another cookie dropped to the pan with a soft sound.

"So go the party. Play hero. You know you want to." Jasmine swiped her finger in the bowl, pulling some raw cookie dough onto her finger, her eyes shutting in pleasure as she licked it off.

Cassius could hear a small choking sound from Taj in the living room, and he rolled his eyes. As bristling as Taj could be, there was at least *one* person who could soften his edges.

Cassius wished that he could have someone the way Taj had Jasmine. The way his father, Lucius, had his human mother, Isabella, before the siring. Before their lives had disintegrated into pain, and betrayal.

"I do not *play* hero, why does everyone keep saying that?" Cassius grumbled as he pulled the bowl away from Jasmine.

She frowned.

"If you continue to eat my cookie dough, there will be no cookies to eat, Jasmine." He raised an eyebrow at her.

Jasmine chuckled lightly.

"Just go to the party. Let loose a little too, while you're at it. Have some fun." She waggled her eyebrows at Cassius who huffed a sigh of exasperation.

"One can hardly have fun when there

is danger lurking in the shadows." He shoved the tray of raw cookies into the oven.

Jasmine rolled her eyes.

"Always so dramatic."

Cassius's eyes met Taj's.

"I will go. But I can guarantee I will *not* have *fun*."

***

Cassius held the coffee in one hand and a bag of cookies in the other. Yet, he felt strangely nervous in a way he hadn't felt since he was a young teenager.

Ava sat with her back against a tree in the quad, and she looked rather spent. He could see even at a distance, the bags underneath her eyes, and the deep breaths she was taking. She looked tired, and most certainly in need of caffeine and sugar. Women loved caffeine and sugar, and he prayed she would too. Each step he took toward her felt like a canyon, but he kept going. Her eyes opened, eyelashes fluttering in the shade as he approached her.

"You must have a death wish," she drawled as he came to the edge of the shaded tree, his shoes barely touching the edge of her boots.

"Perhaps it is you who has the death wish." He held out the coffee.

"What is this?" She looked up at him skeptically.

"A peace offering." He nodded at her.

"What's in the bag?" Her eyes glanced down to his fingers that held the bag shut, and he could not deny the way they fixated on his slender wrist.

This close to her he could feel her

heightened pulse, and he wondered what she was thinking about.

The sun hit him at his back, and he felt flush and warm, between its heat and the vibrating pulse of his marked human. Never in a million years did Cassius think he would have marked *anyone*. But he had, and he knew because of his actions, it would be rather difficult to stay away. He needed to be near her, if only to keep an eye on her. To make sure she was safe. He had vowed to do so, and he intended to keep his word. Even if being near her put him in danger.

Mal had relented, but he knew it may only be a matter of time before the hunter found a way to discard him. It was what he did.

Kill people like Cassius.

"Chocolate chip cookies." He handed her the bag, and she took it, her fingers brushing his lightly, sending a jolt of electricity through him.

The touch felt so...*good*, but it was rather short lived.

Ava opened the bag and peered in, as if expecting a spider or something to jump out and scare her. "A peace offering, huh? How do I know you didn't poison this shit, and this is how I end up in your fucking lair?"

"I suppose you'll just to have to trust me." He smiled, trying to look as innocent as possible.

"What kind of drink is that?" She looked up at him.

"Coffee."

"Black?" she asked as she wrinkled her nose.

"Heavens, no. No sane human drinks black coffee." The wind rustled his hair, and he could feel her pulse start to race once more. He held the coffee out to her.

She took it from his hands and set it on the ground.

He slid his hands in his pockets, and she pulled a cookie from the bag, looking it over with suspicion before taking the smallest bite.

"Thank you. For the other night," he spoke.

"Like I said, we're even now." She took another bite.

"Please don't go to the party," he pleaded.

"Is this why you brought me sweet treats? Try and butter me up? Did you think if you bought me food I'd just agree to your demands?"

I had hoped so, yes.

As she said the words, Cassius could feel his own dark blood start to heat. It sounded like bribery.

It wasn't *not* bribery.

Suddenly he felt on the spot. "I am not demanding anything of you, I just—"

"Good. Because I don't like to be told what the fuck to do." She rose from her seat, bag and coffee in hand. She took a step closer to him. "Especially by bloodthirsty killing machines who wear leather pants when its eighty-five fucking degrees." She brushed past him.

"What's wrong with my pants?" Cassius felt perplexed as he watched her saunter off.

"See you around, Cas." She waved to him as she walked off.

"Thanks for the poison," were the last

words she spoke before she disappeared around the corner.

CHAPTER THIRTY-TWO

AVA WALKED PAST the array of shops on Main Street, her hands in her jeans pocket. It was still early afternoon, and due to Hunter wrapping up whatever it was Mal and the others had assisted him with, Dallas was occupied. She wasn't angry, jealous, or perturbed by any means. She understood the relationships between Mal and his best friend, and even the other hunters as she'd observed, was something that had been built over several years. They had a bond, the five of them. A bond that was born of blood, and death.

After all, it wasn't as if she and Dallas were...anything really. They'd kissed, sure. But that didn't mean they were together or anything.

She'd just lost her boyfriend. It was a moment of weakness, a moment of just...

Being able to forget. A moment of lust, nothing more.

But she couldn't deny that she enjoyed the moment. She enjoyed it quite a bit more than she probably should have.

Just remembering the feeling of his hands running up her back, his arousal pressed against her... The way his stubble brushed her skin as he ran his tongue up her jaw... And the fight beforehand hadn't been without its charms either.

Then there was Cassius.

A part of her felt guilty, it had been his image that filled her brain as she kissed Dallas, but she was also thankful that he was able to redirect her desires, if only for a moment.

She didn't want to think about Cassius. About his deep green eyes, his perfect model face, or his sharp fangs.

Or the fact that he had brought her a *peace offering.* Whatever that fucking meant.

He was a vampire. A monster.

The enemy.

Cookies and coffee didn't change that. It never would.

She was grateful he had saved her,

but she was also angry.

He certainly didn't have time to explain but...

It still felt unfair. He'd asked her permission, but how was she to know what he was truly asking? He may have saved her life, but she knew as she looked up at him amidst the daylight, that it was much more complicated than that.

Her hair blew in her face, and she remembered the night before, with Dallas. How easy it had been to wade into those waters. How, for only a moment, she had forgotten about all of it. How the fight had transpired into something else when Dallas pulled her by her long, sweat soaked ponytail into his hard embrace.

Even though it had led to a most

enjoyable, hot make out session, she had to admit if Dallas could use her long, silken locks against her, perhaps a vampire such as Cas may be able to do the same.

She stopped in front of Lori's Hair Salon, her reflection catching in the window. She'd never *cut* her hair before. She'd had plenty of trims, to keep it long and luscious. It looked so pretty when she'd tie it back, especially with a bow when she donned her cheerleading uniform. But it had started to become a nuisance.

Always flying around in the wind, sticking to her lip gloss. It took nearly an hour to wash and dry every day.

And it could be the difference between life and death, quite literally.

When Lori took the scissors to her

hair, Ava closed her eyes. She couldn't bear to watch the years of growth tumble to the floor. When she opened her eyes finally and looked in the mirror, she felt a sting of panic.

Lori brushed and straightened her shoulder length locks, and Ava couldn't deny a sense of excitement swelled in her stomach. It brought forth a feeling of newness, of confidence she hadn't quite expected.

She couldn't stop looking at her reflection in the shop windows she passed, getting used to the new person she looked like. Which was why she was taken by surprise when she ran into a short, familiar red-headed individual.

"I'm so sorry... Ava?" Ember spoke in surprise.

"I uh...didn't see you there, Em,

sorry." Ava chuckled.

"You...cut your hair?" Ember raised an eyebrow.

"Yeah, it was getting to be a pain in the ass, so..."

Ember smiled.

"Do you like it?" Ava asked, running her fingers through the shorter locks. It still felt odd, the quick feeling, because of where it stopped, just brushing her shoulder with its edges.

"I do." Ember smiled.

"Where you headed at this hour?" she asked Ava.

"Nowhere, really, I was just...walking. Getting fresh air,"

Getting my mind off the inevitable.

The party was in two days. She was nervous.

She longed to use her stake, to be

able to bring justice to Ross, herself, and the victims of the vampires, but...

What if I choke?

What if all this training, all of this...what if I can't do it?

Ava pushed the thoughts from her mind. She couldn't think that way. If she did, she'd be dead. But she was still nervous. She supposed nerves would not relent until she'd followed through.

Until she'd put the monsters six feet under.

Or more accurately, burned them to ash.

You won't be alone, you will have back up.

While Dallas had said he'd back her up, Mal would not hear the word *no* on the matter either.

With the two of them in the same

vicinity, she felt better, but she also felt as if it was more important than ever to show them, she was capable of this on her own.

"Are you going to the party up at the old stone church on sixty?" Ember asked.

"Yeah, why?" Her shoulders tensed. "You're not considering going, are you?" Her blood chilled. Ember was not the type to attend parties of any kind, but Ava *had* suggested on more than one occasion that Ember needed to socialize more. Although, she hoped her friend hadn't taken up on her suggestion so soon.

"Ava, you know you can talk to me, right?" Ember reached out and ran her hand on Ava's arm. "You don't have to throw yourself into partying, or drinking or..."

Ava could feel the smile forming on her lips. "I know, Em. But I'm not the kind of person who's going to sit around and mope. You know me. I need to move. I need to be where the action is," she said.

I need to drive a stake through the vampire that killed my boyfriend, and the one who almost killed me.

The two of them walked down the street together, past The Third Eye, the metaphysical shop in which Ava worked and Ember frequented. It was how they met. It had been mere coincidence that Ember and Ava had ended up in the same medieval history class together.

"I know I just..."

"I know. And I appreciate it." Ava nudged her shoulder as they stopped in front of one of the town's most popular clothing boutiques, which was all done up and decorated with Halloween costumes and merchandise for the impending holiday. Tiny red and orange leaves bristled about Ava's ankles, and a shiver ran down her spine. The temperature was starting to drop, and the sun was starting to disappear into the clouds. It would soon be night.

"Are you going to dress up?" Ember twisted her lips as she looked at the display case full of short costumes.

"I haven't given it much thought, actually."

"You could always go as a college kid," Ember said, deadpan. "Wouldn't have to buy a costume." She laughed awkwardly.

Ava rolled her eyes. "What's the point

of dressing up on Halloween if you're just going to go as something you can go as every day of the year?" She looked in the display case of the boutique, which still showcased some regular clothes amidst the pleated skirts and cleavage bearing costumes. Her eyes settled on a thick, black leather jacket with studs on the collar.

Looking at it gave her an instant smile.

I bet that would look badass with all my band tees.

But it was another thought that sparked her interest more.

I bet I could hide a stake in there.

CHAPTER THIRTY-THREE

THE CHURCH ON route sixty had been abandoned for nearly fifty years. The only life it saw was a few drifters, perhaps some thrill-seeking teenagers. It certainly hadn't housed more than a small handful of individuals at once, let alone a smattering of college students all looking to lose themselves in liquor and sex.

Cassius and Tajiri stood on the edge

of the rock terrain, the sound of music loud amidst the chatter. Even outside, Cassius could smell the scents of alcohol, sweat, and mildew.

Liam and his cohorts were inside, he knew that.

But so was Ava.

He could feel her pulse beating steadily, and he knew she was near, and that made him feel quite the mixture of emotion.

Taj smiled as he headed toward the main doors, past the scantily dressed angels and demons loitering about the entrance.

How fitting.

Upon opening the door, he was assaulted with a hundred scents: from the crowd of bodies dancing, drinking.

Candles were lit all about; on the

dusty altar, in the entryway on cobwebbed tables, in the crevices of windowsills lighting up the expanse of stained-glass windows.

Taj moved quickly, in search of his target, and Cassius tried to keep up, but he couldn't deny that the sight brought back memories he hadn't expected.

Memories of another life.

Eden ran her fingernails down his face, over the throbbing vein in his neck.

Her teeth nipped at his lower lip, and he could still taste blood on the edge of her fangs as his own tongue stroked hers in response.

The candles flickered against the stained-glass windows, all shades of orange against the red painted glass.

The Boracelli's always did have quite the flair for drama.

His tongue licked at her fangs, the taste of blood making him long for more.

Eden giggled, and the sound was both haunting and melodic.

Cassius shook the memories from his mind, as he pushed his way through the crowd, the pulse in his veins getting stronger with each stride.

He watched the crowd, and noted Tajiri was moving faster. He could smell the overbearing musk of Liam, and knew he was close as well.

Then his gaze settled on her.

She stood in the center of the room, her arms around Liam's neck. She looked...different.

Clad in a leather jacket, and a black corseted costume dress, pale legs standing out against the darkness. He could see her black boots came up to her mid-thigh, elongating the slender shape of her legs. Her hair was shorter, angled close to her shoulders, and the ruby red stain on her lips flared his thirst.

It was just makeup, he knew that.

But it drove thoughts of blood and lust through his brain in a way he hadn't felt since he'd fully transitioned.

Liam smiled, the motion showcasing his fangs, and Ava let her head roll back.

Liam leaned his lips against her collarbone, and Cassius moved with heightened purpose. Thunder roared above the music and chatter, shaking the unsteady ground.

Ava ran her hands down Liam's arms, her fingers intertwining with his.

She glanced up in that moment, and their eyes met as the rain fell hard against the roof.

CHAPTER THIRTY-FOUR

IT WAS MUCH easier than she had anticipated, finding Liam. Now that she knew what he was, she trusted her newly found vampiric radar would steer her in the right direction. When she'd told Mal about her suspicions, he'd confirmed the truth. According to lore, and several firsthand accounts of victims, some survivors as well, the marked could sense not only *their* vampire's presence, but that it was nearly impossible to distinguish the vampire who marked them, from any *other* vampire.

"It could be useful for us," Dallas had suggested.

Mal did not want to agree, but Ava felt the same way. While Dallas and Mal, and likely the other hunters as well had trained, and were probably so good at tracking a vamp they could do it their sleep, Ava had to admit it would be rather helpful, and time saving if she could just...follow her vampire radar right into the hands of the monster.

And that is exactly what she did. She hadn't told Mal or Dallas her plan, knowing that both of them would likely try to talk her out of such things, but she knew they were close. If they were concerned something would go south, they'd come to her rescue.

But things would *not* go that way. She would not let them. She'd remain in control. She'd focus her mind. She'd find a way. Failure was just not an option.

And it seemed her plan was working. Liam took her bait like a moth to a flame. His thrall reached out around her, and she could feel the faint cloudiness in her brain, but it wasn't as mind numbing as she'd been told. Either that, or Liam was not running at full power, which she did not intend to push.

She felt *him,* before she saw him.

Not only did her skin prickle with goosebumps, her wrist flare with heat, but her blood *heated* in a way it hadn't when she approached Liam.

Like it knew somehow, someway…it

was *his.*

She pushed the thought down vehemently. No one owned her body, her blood. Or any part of her, truly.

She could feel his gaze on her, and the memory of the night he bit her once again forged through the walls of her mind. She closed her eyes for a moment, rolling her head back, and Liam's lips brushed her collarbone. His thrall dissipated, and she knew he thought he had her.

That she was just a victim like the others, so he pulled back.

That will be your first mistake, fucking leech.

When she opened her eyes, she caught Cassius's gaze. He stood only mere feet away, but it might as well have been a vast canyon. His golden blonde hair rustled slightly from the motion of young collegiate drunkenly bumping into him, and he was wearing a simple heathered grey shirt, and those same black leather pants he'd had on the other day.

What, do they assign you a fucking uniform or something when you graduate vampire academy or some shit?

Though she couldn't deny the look wasn't a bad one for him.

He moved closer, and she knew he intended to sweep in and disrupt her plan. Which she could not let him do. Not if she wanted to stake Liam, and the one who'd slit her thighs, leaving a nasty scar.

She pulled Liam, breaking Cassius's gaze as she found her way through the crowd of people, moving quickly so as to lose Cassius in the sea of costumed students.

Liam stopped in his tracks, his eyes alert and she stopped too, looking around to see if perhaps there was something she'd missed. Or someone.

"Logan..." Liam's voice carried the hint of concern.

"There's been a...complication..." This Logan looked at Ava quickly, before continuing.

"It's hunters," she heard him whisper.

Fuck.

A hand touched the small of her back, sliding around her hip, pulling her away from Liam

No...

She turned slightly, to see pale blue eyes staring down at her.

"Hey, baby, I've been looking

everywhere for you." His voice was solid, and she knew it was just an act, but she couldn't help the flutter in her heart at his words.

Not now, Ava. Now is not the time...

She scanned the crowd once more, but Cassius was gone.

"Liam..." Logan's eyes cast a glare at Dallas, whose hand had made its way into his back pocket.

Ava leaned lightly, glancing at his ass. He held against himself something with the slightest silver sheen—a knife.

"Care to introduce me to your friend, Ava?" Liam spoke, and she could feel the beginnings of thrall seeping out, much more powerful now.

Her head started to feel...foggy.

Dallas tightened his grip on her.

"I think we're well past

introductions," he answered

Liam glanced at Logan, and back at Ava.

"I will have to catch up with you later, Ava." Liam licked his lips.

When he left, Ava felt as if the world was spinning. Her legs felt slightly like Jell-O.

Dallas braced her against his arm, and for the moment she was glad for the support, but once the fog settled the anger pushed forth.

"What the fuck, Dallas!" She moved out of his touch and shoved him.

"I had him!" she spat.

"Bullshit, Ava, he had *you*." Dallas slid his knife back into his pocket.

"I was this fucking close to staking him!" She glared at him. "And you let him fucking go!"

"Look around, Ava. We're in a crowded room. Full of witnesses. If you want to fucking end this sucker you need to get him alone where no one can see." He pursed his lips.

"That's what I *was* doing before you so rudely interrupted me." She crossed her arms.

"You cut your hair..." Dallas reached out, running his fingers through the edges and she brushed him off.

"Don't, Dallas," she growled as she shoved past him with fury.

"Where the fuck you think you're going?" he bit back.

"To kill a fucking vampire. On my own!"

Dallas was at her back, pulling on her wrist. She yanked her arm out of his grip.

"Ava..."

Thunder boomed in the distance, rattling the windows.

She could hear the sound of a struggle beyond the doors of the crowd.

The sound of glass shattering, of a pained scream.

And upon hearing that scream, it all came back.

Ross's moan of pleasure, the scream of pain.

The knife cutting through her flesh.

Cassius's fangs in her skin.

All of it.

Ava didn't think twice about running into the shadows, leaving Dallas behind.

CHAPTER THIRTY-FIVE

TAJ AND LIAM struggled in what Cassius assumed must have once been the office of the church. The two vampires knocked into everything, fangs snapping, fingers grasping at throats. Old, worn and musty smelling papers flew about like confetti in the dank room.

Cassius knew better than to try and break up the fight, knowing Taj finally had his target. Before he'd followed Taj into the office, there was a man who showed up, who broke the thrall of Liam, who pulled Ava's attention from *him*.

But he hadn't intended on having to put up a fight of his own against Logan, the man who'd pulled Liam's attention from Ava.

And by the looks of it, he was a hunter too.

The way in which the tall, muscular man touched Ava ignited a spark of jealousy in Cassius. Which was an odd feeling altogether.

He barely knew Ava, but the sight of this man with his hands on her...

He'd known she had a boyfriend. For God's sakes, the night he saved her...

She'd asked him to save her *boyfriend*.

He'd just attended the funeral for the man, after all.

Cassius was no stranger to loss, and understood everyone processed their grief differently, but he couldn't help but feel that perhaps this man, this hunter with Ava... Perhaps he was taking advantage of said grief, and that angered Cassius.

But he had no time to *play hero,* as Jasmine would say. Not when the scent of Liam hit his nose, and Tajiri went running after it. Not when Logan swung at him, his fist connecting with Cassius's jaw, fangs bared in a lethal hiss.

That was the second time in a week Cassius had been punched. He hoped this would not become a habit, or a side effect of around Ava. Though, even if it was, he would endure it. It wasn't just the mark on her, though. That was a large part of things, but—

She intrigued him in a way most people didn't.

Just as Cassius bared his fangs against Logan, scrappling against the man's hard chest, the sound of the door crashing open pulled all of their attention.

Mal stood in the doorway, purple and blue lights from the church's main worshipping room lighting him up, his cursed knife glinting off the neon light behind him, and the dark look in his chocolate eyes was a familiar one Cassius had only just discovered in recent days.

The man who'd been behind Ava before was behind Mal now.

Which meant Ava was alone, and

Brody was still out there.

Cassius pushed against Logan, delivering a swift punch to his jaw, the sound of cracking prevalent in the air as he channeled his strength and forced Logan up and backward into the wall.

The perks of being a vampire if there were any, included the reserves of strength he hadn't possessed as seeming mortal.

Though a born vampire such as Cassius tended to have more abilities than that of sired vampires, in this moment he was particularly glad for it.

His eyes locked with Mal, who grinned sadistically.

"Well, well, look what we have here, Dallas,"

The man behind Mal had a name.

Dallas.

Tajiri bared his fangs at the hunters, and despite the fact they were fighting their own enemies, suddenly it was as if the lines were crystal clear. Vampires united against the humans that threatened to kill them.

But Cassius did not want to *kill* anyone.

He felt on the precipice of something greater.

He'd had quite the history of caring for mortals, that was his immortal curse. There had been plenty of mortals he'd called friends; those who he'd defended.

Protected.

So, he recognized the look in Mal's face.

Undying loyalty, sworn to protect those close to them.

But he would not let anything, or

anyone come between him and the woman who bore his claim on her blood. It went against his vampiric instincts, but furthermore, he knew he would not let anyone come between him and the woman he swore to protect, the first person in over a century who'd made him *feel something.*

Alive.

And so, as Tajiri and Liam fought against the oversized Dallas, Cassius called forth on his reserves and bared his fangs at Mal.

"I am not your enemy, Malcolm. You do not have to do this." His eyes fixed on Mal's sinister stare.

"You are the very definition of my enemy, *Cassius.*" Mal stepped forward.

"I do not wish to hurt you."

"Pity, because I'm going to make you

wish for death, you fucking parasite."

Mal swung his arm out, and Cassius instinctively shielded himself from the impact of the blade. The sharp tip cut into his palm, stinging his flesh. Dark, thick black liquid seeped out of his hand.

His blood—black as night.

"You have left her in danger, he is still out there," Cassius growled at Mal, who broke his hold, attempting to get closer.

The sound of agony raged behind him, and the scent of decay and death was prevalent.

Burning.

Cassius did not want to look away from Mal, worried the slight distraction would give Mal an advantage, but he had to know.

His gaze raked over the scene behind him, and Liam's bones disintegrated before his eyes. Tajiri roared against Dallas, and the two fighting together looked rather like two large wrestlers going at it in the ring. They were both men of a certain size, more muscle than was necessary.

Cassius's veins *throbbed*, and his skin felt like ice.

He could feel her. She was close, and the racing of her pulse caused worry to flash in his eyes.

"Ava is in trouble," he said, hoping to reason with Mal.

"Nice try, bloodsucker—"

"I can *feel* her pulse, she is—"

Mal growled and swung again, knocking Cassius against the desk, angling his body on top of him, rearing his arm back to strike.

Cassius pushed back with all his might, his fingers grasping at Mal's, fighting for the knife.

"We can do this another time, Mal. But right now, I am *not* your enemy. Right now, I am your ally." He knocked Mal backward, casting a glare back at Tajiri who had thwarted off Dallas for the time being.

Dallas ran his hand through his hair, and when he pulled it away, Cassius noted the blood.

The scent of it ignited him, stirred his thirst.

But it didn't smell as appetizing as Ava's had.

He'd gone without fresh blood for so long, and though he hungered for it in this moment, there were more pressing matters. Thank goodness he'd consumed his share of corpse blood before attending this raucous, macabre party.

Cassius took off, following the pulse alive in his veins, with only one purpose, one desire.

To protect what belonged to him.

He didn't even notice two hunters, and a pissed off vampire running behind him.

CHAPTER THIRTY-SIX

THE VAMPIRE WHO'D attacked her bared his fangs at her neck. His thrall seeped into her, and it wasn't an unpleasant feeling. In fact, it was quite a desirable feeling if she was being honest.

Brody pushed her up against the wall in the hallway beside the altar, his hands settling over Ava's ass as she wrapped her legs around him.

Ava couldn't deny the thoughts that

forged through at his actions, and had she been completely in her right mind, she knew she should be disgusted at the thought.

She closed her eyes, and for the moment it wasn't Brody and his creeping hands over her body, wasn't his fangs poised at her neck.

No, instead her psyche kicked up the image of a rather appealing blond vampire with glowing green eyes, and the thought of *his* fangs in her neck...

She tightened her legs around Brody and let out a deep moan. Her eyes fluttered, and the light from the altar filtered through, and she felt the brush of something sharp against her thigh.

A stake.

Suddenly awash with realization of what was happening, Ava remembered where she was, and what she came to do.

Her brain pushed away all thoughts of Cassius, and the memory of Ross, of the knife in her skin, of her parent's bloodied bodies on the floor reared its ugly head and suddenly nothing was clearer.

Ava continued to play the part as she slid her hand down her thigh, moaning in delight for Brody's ears.

It wasn't *entirely* a lie. What he was doing *did* in fact feel good, but it was his thrall, a natural defense. It wasn't as if she was attracted to the man who sliced her legs open and left her to die.

That would be highly fucked up.

Brody's tongue licked the skin on her neck, right over her throbbing vein.

"I've never stolen someone's mark

before. This is going to be—"

Ava slid the stake out of her garter underneath her skirt. Her arms felt like Jell-O, but she forced the movements anyway, and then she felt *him.*

Her wrist flared with heat; her skin chilled like ice.

Her blood heating in response to his presence.

Cassius.

Though she wanted to, she was certain she could *not* look at him right now.

If she did, she'd lose her concentration, her nerve.

Her focus.

Ava's nerves stood on edge, and her breathing caught in her throat.

Images of tongues on skin battled with the sounds of pained screams, and

Ava felt the rush of adrenaline surging through her as she brought her stake to Brody's chest.

At the realization of what she was doing, he growled at her, grabbing her harder, ready to bite.

She fought against him, and she could *feel* Cassius as he approached her.

"Stay the hell away from me!" she roared at him

"Ava—" His voice was soft, and warm, and she refused to let it drive the images she fought so hard against.

"I mean it, Cas!"

Familiar voices echoed in the distance against the muffled music, and she knew them well.

Dallas, and Mal.

Ava and Brody wrestled against one another. Ava struck out once more with her stake, but Brody, wise to her goal, stopped it.

Everything was a blur of rage. Fists flying, backs knocking against the wall. Her arm braced against something sharp, and she could feel the rush of blood to the surface, and it only fueled her more.

Ava breathed heavily as adrenaline coursed through her, and Cassius was at her side almost as soon as her back hit the wall, but his existence next to her was short lived as Mal grabbed him, pulling him away.

"Don't even fucking think about it—" Mal wrapped his arms around Cassius, and Ava noted he only struggled a little bit. As if he was glad Mal held him captive. Which was odd.

It was the distraction she needed.

She leapt for Brody and kicked his legs out from under him. He went down with a thud and Ava wasted no time straddling him with her legs. The very one's he'd cut open with knives.

Brody tried to use his thrall, but even his vampire jedi mind tricks were no match for the feeling of power she felt at the moment.

Holding his cursed life in her hands.

Being able to prevent so much death, with just one plunge of an ash wood stake.

"You fucking bitch," he snarled. "I should have killed you when I had the chance." He fought against her hold, but with all the adrenaline running through her body, her force was stronger than she anticipated.

"Yeah, you should have." She smiled

as she pulled her stake back. "But you picked the wrong girl to fuck over, buddy." And without hesitation, she plunged her stake into his chest.

He recoiled around her, letting out a deep growl that sounded all too much like thunder.

The sounds of the party roared in the background, and spurts of dark, black liquid erupted from his chest, splashing her hands and arms, and a stray drop even hit her face.

It felt like blood, but it looked like...

Oil. Sludge.

Vampires have...blood?

The question pushed forth, but she did not have time to be curious. She needed to light the vampire in front of her on fire if she wanted him to truly stay dead.

She slid her hands in her back skirt pocket, reaching for the set of matches Dallas had given her. The world around her fell silent as she focused on the strike of the match, the smell of sulfur. She rose from his body quickly as the match hit him, pulling the stake from his chest with her.

As she stood, she could feel her blood hot like flowing lava in a volcano.

Her eyes found Cassius's as Brody's body gave way to flames, skin and muscle disappearing, bones crumbling like kindling in a fireplace.

The look in Cassius's eyes was dark, but there was a hint of something else she couldn't place.

Ava nodded at Mal, who looked surprised.

But he let him go all the same.

With the high she was feeling right now, she felt as if she could take on anyone.

Anything.

Cassius glanced at her only for a moment before taking off in the shadows.

CHAPTER THIRTY-SEVEN

CASSIUS WATCHED AS Ava drove the stake into Brody's body with precision and ease. Like it was the most natural thing in the world.

He'd known saving her was the right thing to do. And yet the divide between them was...murky at best when she was *just* a human, and he was just a vampire.

It was more than crystal clear now as

he watched Brody's blood spatter onto her hands, and even a bit on her face.

Ava was a hunter.

It was in her blood, that was more than apparent.

Like her brother.

She killed people like him.

Monsters like him.

Yet as he caught her amber gaze, his entire being was flush with heat at the sight.

Her pulse quickened, her chest heaved, her breasts rising and falling with rapid breath. Images of blood-soaked thighs pushed forth, of fangs buried deep in her neck, and his cock twitched at the thought, the sight.

He was both equally terrified and *proud.*

It wouldn't be the first time he felt

attracted to someone who could kill him.

He caught the slight nod of her head toward Mal.

"This isn't over, Cassius," Mal hoarsely whispered in his ear, before letting go.

Cassius would not waste the chance to escape the hunters.

He needed to find Tajiri, make sure he was all right.

If anything had happened to him...

Cassius passed Ava and nodded in her direction before disappearing into the shadowed hall in search of his friend.

***

Taj collapsed on the couch in a heap. "Man, I haven't had a fight that heavy in a long time," he grumbled.

Cassius was glad he'd escaped the hunters, although he knew it was likely because the hunters were focused on a different target.

A target with short brown hair, and amber eyes of fire to be exact.

"Yes, well, I fear there may be more brawls in our future," Cassius sighed.

"You can't be serious, Cassius..." Taj ran his hand over his face as Jasmine peeked her head around the corner.

"What's wrong?" she asked inquisitively.

"Ava is—"

"A hunter." Taj finished the words.

Jasmine's eyes widened. "Well, that complicates things a bit, doesn't it?" Jasmine slowly walked up to the couch and took a seat next to Taj.

"A bit, yes," Cassius whispered, his

eyes closing in defeat.

"You need to forget about her, Cassius, for your own good..." Taj's voice held an air of concern and worry.

"I wish it were that simple, Tajiri. I really do," he said as he got up from the couch, suddenly quite exhausted for someone who didn't need to sleep.

Jasmine and Taj did not say anything as he wandered off to his bedroom in search of solace.

CHAPTER THIRTY-EIGHT

THE MEDIA, AND the college lumped Liam, Brody, and Logan's disappearances in conjunction with Ross and the Klume sisters, enflaming the rumors of a serial killer in the town and on campus.

Yet, after a month, the hoopla, as Becky called it, seemed to die down, what with the murders seemingly coming to an end.

Mal had stuck around for the longest time, clear until Thanksgiving, before he'd decided that everything was quiet enough to leave.

Dallas sat in the driver seat of the Chevelle as Mal loaded the last of his suitcases and a clean amp in the back of the car. As Mal headed back indoors to say goodbye, Ava felt it only right to say her own goodbyes.

She leaned her arms on the windowsill.

"Where you two headed?" she asked, trying to focus on anything but the sight of Dallas's lips.

"No destination yet, but I'm sure something will pop up before too long. Lots of monsters out there." He ran his fingers over the side of the steering wheel, his blue eyes catching hers with unspoken words.

"Well, it's been fun." She smirked.

Dallas paused for a moment, his gaze drifting down to her mouth before catching her eyes once more. "That is has, kitten." A faint smile tugged at his lips.

"Try not to get into too much trouble without me." She smiled back.

"You trying to lecture me?" He let out a light chuckle.

"Depends. Do you want me to lecture you?" Her eyes lit up with amusement.

"Fuck no," he said.

Mal walked through the door, making a beeline for the car. He slid into the passenger seat and slapped the dashboard. "I'll try and be back for Christmas." He looked at Ava with slight concern. "But if you need *anything,* and I mean anything..."

"I'll call you, I promise." Ava rolled her eyes.

"Okay." His shoulders eased just a fraction, and Dallas started the car.

"See ya when I see ya," Mal shouted as Dallas backed the car out of the driveway.

Ava watched them drive off, as she had many other times. This time she felt a pang of sadness, but she did not dwell on it. She walked down main street with her hands in her pockets, toward Cory's Diner.

The air was chilly, but she preferred it much more to the blistering heat that was often prevalent even in the autumn in Virginia. It wouldn't be long before snow finally made its appearance, which she also detested. But for the moment, it was a perfect fall afternoon.

She sat on the bench across from Cory's, taking in the sight of the world around her. The few people walking by the light of the neon sign.

A light fluttering sounded beside her, and her wrist flared with heat.

Goosebumps erupted on her skin.

"You must have a death wish. Clearly that, or you are certifiably insane." She turned her glance to Cassius.

"I can assure you I have exquisite mental awareness, my sweet Avarice." His lips bore the ghost of a smile.

"That's not my name." She shifted her body, the motion causing her legs to bristle against his.

"I know." He leaned back against the bench, crossing his ankles.

Silence fell between them.

"I could kill you, you know," she whispered.

"I know," was all he said.

But today would not be that day, she knew that.

Though death was inevitable.

It would either be hers...or his.

And Ava Crowley had no intention of dying.

Thank you for reading!

***

Ava and Cassius will be back in Blood & Lust: Ava Crowley, Vampire Slayer, #2

Turn the page for a preview from Blood & Lust: Ava Crowley, Vampire Slayer, #2...

PREVIEW

**Some people run from danger...
Ava Crowley flirts with it.**

When Ava and her vampire slayer brother, Mal, embark on a trip to a horror movie convention in Oklahoma for some vital sibling bonding, chaos follows. The kind that requires back up from a band of familiar vampire hunters—including the sexy, sinful Jake Dallas.

Ava soon finds herself flirting with danger in the form of a renowned demonologist with mysterious ties to TerrorCon and the missing girls.

But Ava and the hunters aren't the only ones called to crack the case.

Cassius receives a call from an old friend and is pulled back into a world he's long forgotten. A world of blood, lust, and death. In order to help clear his friend's name, he must find the one responsible for the killings of the innocent girls in the shadows of Oklahoma—all while fighting the magnetic bond between him and the snarky vampire slayer he has undoubtedly fallen in love with over the last two years.

Ava and Cassius must work together to solve the case, but will they be able to fight temptation in the middle of nowhere surrounded by blood and lust?

CHAPTER ONE

AVA WATCHED THE doorstep from afar, from the comforts of inside her Chevy Impala. She leaned one arm on the window, her cheek resting on her fist, while she stretched her other hand out, fingers tapping against the steering wheel.

She'd expected more...something.

Everything seemed quiet in the sleepy town of Chester.

The town was no longer the center of media frenzy.

Sure, there were still *murders*, but nothing quite as scandalous as attractive college kids with strange marks on their thighs and necks like the Chester Murders two years ago.

She could have sworn the man she'd followed had *all* the signs of a vampire, and even if she didn't believe it to be so, her vampire radar never lied.

The bite mark she'd sustained only two years prior, the bite that saved her life—flared with heat while her skin prickled with goosebumps every time a vampire was near.

As if she could have willed it with thought alone, her wrist heated, and a soft knocking on her passenger window alerted her. Her lips twisted in annoyance as a rather attractive blond with a penchant for leather pants smirked at her.

Cassius.

"What do you want?" she bit as she tried to look around him.

"May I come in?" He held a coffee in his hand.

Though she knew she should say no, she could not bring herself to do so, and that aggravated her.

"If it means you are no longer going to obstruct my vision, then yes, by all means, enter my humble abode," she drawled sarcastically as she heard the click of a door.

Cassius opened the door and slid into the passenger seat, the motion elongating his long legs, accentuating the curve of his ass in his black leather pants.

Ava pretended not to notice. Especially when her blood *heated* at the sight.

Cassius offered her the coffee cup. "I was once told never to attend a stake out without coffee."

Ava raised an eyebrow as she took the cup from his hands quickly, opening the lid. The scent of vanilla and cream was divine. "I was told never to invite a vampire into your house or car, yet here we are." She took a sip of the piping hot beverage and had to admit it was divine. "Thanks for the poison, but you didn't have to—"

"I was in the neighborhood." Cassius's eyes sparkled with amusement.

"Uh huh. Sure..." Ava rolled her eyes

in response, focusing on the doorstop.

Nothing. No movement.

Cassius leaned back in the seat casually.

"What if he does not show?" His voice was smooth, like caramel.

"He'll show," she answered as she took another drink of the sweet liquid.

"But if he does not..."

"Then I go home," she grumbled.

"But you will not rest, will you Ava?"

She closed her eyes, letting the coffee warm her insides. She refused the idea that anything but the coffee could warm her like *this*. "Until I put a stake through his chest, you mean? No I won't."

Cassius sighed, turning his head to look out the window. "Well, I suppose we wait then."

"There is no *we*, Cassius. This is my

life, and—" The door budged, and Ava sat straighter. "Bingo," she said as she set down her coffee, turning her car off.

OTHER BOOKS BY ARIEL DAWN

The Hunter Games

Blood Of My Enemy

Blood Of The Lost

Thorne Of Blood

Speed Dating with the Denizens of the Underworld Series

Hecate

Hades

Orion

Athena

Spike

The Forevermore Series

In The Cards

In The Blood

In The Shadows

BLOOD & BONES

In The Deep

In The Garden

In The Night-coming soon!

Shifters Of Starfall Creek Series

Hollow's Sunrise

Hollow's Sunset

Hollow's Legacy

Shifters of Starfall Creek Collection:

Books 1-3

Get a copy of Ariel Dawn's short story,

Faded, when you sign up for her

newsletter!

https://mailchi.mp/e5f326e433bf/dawn

-breaks-official-newsletter

CONNECT WITH ARIEL DAWN

Website

http://www.ariel-dawn.com/

Goodreads:

http://www.goodreads.com/authorariel

dawn

Bookbub:

http://www.bookbub.com/authors/ariel

-dawn

Facebook:

http://www.facebook.com/authorarielda

wn

Twitter:

https://twitter.com/ArielDawn10

Join Dusk Chasers—Ariel Dawn's Official Readers Group for access to exclusive content!

ABOUT ARIEL DAWN

USA TODAY BESTSELLING AUTHOR Ariel Dawn grew up as an avid reader and is a creative soul.

What started out as writing reviews for indie romance authors led to featuring quirky, stereotypical, and weird covers on her Instagram Wrong Turn Romance, which gave her the courage to finally decide to live her dream and become an author.

Ariel writes plot driven paranormal romance and hopes to venture into fantasy and rom-com in the future. When she isn't writing, she can be found cosplaying, attending conventions, creating all sorts of artwork in her studio, or editing photos for her photography business.

A self-professed geek and foodie, she loves hanging out with family and friends and playing video games and board games with her retro gamer husband.